Pursuing Sherlock Holmes

Pursuing Sherlock Holmes

*To Bob & Susan,
With thanks for your friendship and all best wishes.
Bill Mason
9-26-2010*

Bill Mason

Copyright © 2010 by Bill Mason.

Library of Congress Control Number:		2010908555
ISBN:	Hardcover	978-1-4535-2036-9
	Softcover	978-1-4535-2035-2
	Ebook	978-1-4535-2037-6

All rights reserved. No part of this book may be reproduced or transmitted in any form or by any means, electronic or mechanical, including photocopying, recording, or by any information storage and retrieval system, without permission in writing from the copyright owner.

Some elements of this book are fiction. Names, characters, places and incidents either are the product of the author's imagination or are used fictitiously, and any resemblance to any actual persons, living or dead, events, or locales is entirely coincidental.

This book was printed in the United States of America.

To order additional copies of this book, contact:
Xlibris Corporation
1-888-795-4274
www.Xlibris.com
Orders@Xlibris.com
82358

Contents

Young Adventures and Old Cases 9

Trailblazers in the World of Ideas 18
    Sherlock Holmes and the Poets Laureate

My Arrangement with Mr. Holmes 25
    by Mrs. Neville St. Clair

Sightings at Twilight... 33

A Chill on the Moor... 35
    Sex and Sadism in The Hound of the Baskervilles

Horror of the Hound... 48

The Rule of Three 53
    The Significance of Sherlockian Trios

Deeper Shades 64
    The Dressing-Gowns of Sherlock Holmes and the Psychology of Color

Leading with the Chin.. 85
    Careful Considerations Concerning Canonical Chins

Doctor Sterndale, the African Explorer 92

A Tale from the Crypt... 99
    Unearthing Dracula in Sherlock Holmes

A Musical Toast to Nathan Garrideb 114

Between the Lines.. 116
    Thoughts on Sherlock Holmes and Two Remarkable Women

Dead? Not Hardly! 120

Notes 127

Index 145

DEDICATION

To my wife, Cindy,
who always has supported and encouraged me
as I have pursued Sherlock Holmes.

SHOUT-OUTS

To Brad Keefauver,
the innovative genius of the Sherlockian world,
the first to publish any of my writings about the writings.

To Billy Fields and Gael Stahl
and the Nashville Scholars of the Three-Pipe Problem,
who long have carried the banner of Sherlock Holmes in Tennessee.

To Peter Blau,
who has never failed to be responsive or helpful
with my questions and requests concerning Sherlock Holmes.

Young Adventures and Old Cases

When *The Adventures of Sherlock Holmes* were written in 1891 and 1892, Arthur Conan Doyle was in his early thirties—a young man, athletic, with a lifetime still before him. He was full of the enthusiasms of that stage of life. No wonder, then, that all twelve of *The Adventures* contain characters who, like himself, were young and spirited. Every successful writer and every critic recognizes that an author does best when he writes about what he knows. Consciously or unconsciously, the youthful Conan Doyle or the also-youthful narrator of his tales, Dr. John H. Watson, were likely to include such personalities in the exciting tales that made Sherlock Holmes a household word.

Just as a strain of youth and vigor runs through the very first collection of twelve stories about the master detective, a contrary strain of age and frailty runs through *The Case-Book of Sherlock Holmes*. This last collection—also composed of twelve stories—was written between 1923 and 1927, when Conan Doyle was in his mid-sixties. In the last decade of his life, he was tired of Sherlock Holmes, and his enthusiasms had changed dramatically (although they had not disappeared). No wonder, then, that older men—characters who were weary, stooped, or even bitter—were featured in each tale. Older, wiser, and used to the idea that much in the world cannot be changed, the author once again included personalities more aligned with his own perspective on life.

A curious mirror image is reflected in these two sets of twelve stories—a distant reflection of the march of time in the world of Sherlock Holmes as well as in the life of his creator. In each are four suitors and husbands, four family relations, and four specialists in their respective fields.

Suitors and Husbands

None of the four male romantic figures of *The Adventures of Sherlock Holmes*—three suitors and one husband—are leading players in the dramas in which they appear, but all are major factors in the outcome. Each of the them seems to be a fine young man, the sort of person most of us would hope to have as a son-in-law. All of them appear to be more than worthy of the affections of their respective heroines, and we can safely assume that all four marriages were happy ones.

Take Godfrey Norton, for instance. He is described as "dark, handsome and dashing." In the estimation of the well-traveled Irene Adler, Godfrey Norton was "a better man" than a king. Such an opinion from the central character of A SCANDAL IN BOHEMIA, a person who herself is held in such high estimation by no less a person than Sherlock Holmes, surely indicates that Norton was a young man of exceptional qualities, refined, and highly intelligent. Adventuress she might be—and such an appellation carried heavy baggage in that era—Irene would be unlikely to accept anything less than top quality when choosing her lifetime partner.

More earthy, but just as remarkable a personality, must have been Frank Moulton of THE NOBLE BACHELOR. Not only did he survive an Apache raid and captivity—and the Apaches of the American southwest were not exactly known for their gentle demeanor, mercy or compassion—he also wasted no time after making his daring escape. He crossed a continent and an ocean to find the woman he loved. He is like a hero from a Western movie, and his story is worthy of any soap opera.

Both Percy Armitage, the fiancé of Helen Stoner of THE SPECKLED BAND, and Mr. Fowler, the fiancé of Alice Rucastle of THE COPPER BEECHES, remained in the background in these two cases of greed and treachery. Their very presence, however, sparked the chain of events which required the intervention of Sherlock Holmes. These two young men were threats, not to the young women they loved, but to their avaricious guardians. Miss Stoner and Miss Rucastle each had money of her own, but a husband would be able to claim control over that income. Such was Victorian law. So Dr. Grimesby Roylott (Helen's step-father) and Jephro Rucastle (Alice's father) took drastic steps to prevent their marriages and keep that money for themselves. Roy100tt chose to commit a direct act of murder. Rucastle used a more indirect, but ultimately an even more cruel, method.

Interestingly, both Roylott and Rucastle acted against the young women rather than against the suitors. Perhaps the "dear" Armitage, who was numbered among the gentry, and the "persevering" Fowler, a seafaring man of sufficient status to merit "a government appointment," were regarded by the schemers as too-powerful adversaries for a direct assault. Both Armitage and Fowler were indeed superior young men. They were above personal defamation, immune to intimidation or bribery, and/

or vigorous enough to resist any physical threat. The villains Roylott and Rucastle were cowards after all, attacking women but avoiding a clash with strong young men.

Contrast these fine specimens—Norton, Moulton, Armitage and Fowler, three suitors and one husband—to four unappealing old fools, three husbands and one suitor, of *The Case-Book of Sherlock Holmes*. Pursuing women young enough to be their daughters, consumed by selfishness and jealousy, and unwilling to acknowledge the unavoidable consequences of age, they are a collective nightmare, all unworthy and ultimately unsuitable for their actual or intended mates, all thoroughly odious.

The most bizarre of these would have to be Professor Presbury of THE CREEPING MAN, the 61-year-old so-called "great scientist" who pursued the young and beautiful Alice Morphy, not with "the reasoned courting of an elderly man but rather the passionate frenzy of youth." For her part, as might be expected, Alice was more interested in men of her own generation. "Age stood in the way," so the professor took drastic action—injections of monkey serum to make him more virile and, presumably, more attractive. Of course, it made him even more ridiculous, affected his mind, and apparently made him stink to the point that his own dog wanted to kill him.

Old men can make bad husbands, at least in the Sherlockian canon. And the consequence of bad old husbands appears to have been consistent—a covert romance and violent death. Interestingly enough, however, the victim was not always the most deserving of that fate. In other words, quite unfortunately, the old coot himself was not the one who paid with his life, as a more cosmic concept of justice might require.

Josiah Amberley of THE RETIRED COLOURMAN, another 61-year-old, retired and "married a woman twenty years younger than himself," apparently hoping for a very pleasurable old age. She, having developed an understandable distaste for her union with "a miser as well as a harsh and exacting husband," allowed her eye to wander. By doing so, she drove this "pathetic, futile, broken creature" to murder. Amberley did nothing by half measures—he stuffed the bodies of his wife and her lover down a well, faked a robbery, concocted and alibi, and even tried to use Sherlock Holmes himself as a red herring.

In another case, Ronder, the circus owner, was "one of the greatest showmen of his day," but his day was long past. His description in THE VEILED LODGER paints a grim picture. He "was a man of many enemies," we are told. "A huge bully of a man, he cursed and slashed at everyone who came in his way." He married a young woman, who, like Mrs. Amberley, had a wandering eye. In Mrs. Ronder's case, her attentions landed on the circus' strong man, Leonardo. Ronder's abusiveness, his wife's unfaithfulness and complicity in murder, and her lover's cowardice populate this tale with some of the most distasteful characters in the canon. In this case, though, justice was served: Ronder was murdered, his wife was maimed, and her lover was drowned. No trio ever so deserved their respective fates.

And Neil Gibson, the "Gold King" of THE PROBLEM OF THOR BRIDGE, was a hardened veteran of life in general. The description provided for Gibson is vivid: "His face might have been chiseled in granite, hard-set, craggy, remorseless, with deep lines upon it, the scars of many a crisis." In many ways, J. Neil Gibson was the worst husband of all, because he inflicted scars of a different kind on others, especially his wife. He was not reacting to unrequited love, as did Amberley or Presbury or perhaps even Ronder. He gave the back of his hand to a very devoted wife and chased after a younger woman. In this case, the most innocent party suffered the most tragic of fates, suicide. It was the last weapon in her arsenal.

Family Relations

As many, if not most, people learn to their eternal disappointment and chagrin, you cannot pick your family. Basically, you are stuck with them. In *The Adventures of Sherlock Holmes*, four of the tales involve young men—three sons and a parasitic step-father—who became part of the narrative mainly because of their relationship with the victim of whatever crime or outrage Holmes was investigating. The one factor they all held in common was that they were thorough underachievers.

James Windibank was actually a young man, "some thirty years of age, clean shaven, and sallow-skinned, with a bland, insinuating manner." In A CASE OF IDENTITY, he managed somehow to marry a woman considerably older than himself; and, in a manner reminiscent of Roylott and Rucastle, determined to hold onto his step-daughter's financial assets. Being "a cold-blooded scoundrel" and knowing that his step-daughter—closer to his own age than was his wife—was naive, severely near-sighted, and plainly a few bricks short of a full load, he was able to woo and deceive her. Holmes was incensed by him, but not to the point, unfortunately that he was motivated to enlighten Miss Sutherland about the deception.

Young Arthur Holder was not morally bankrupt, as was Windibank, despite being somewhat spoiled and "a grievous disappointment" to his father because of his gambling excesses. "He was wild, wayward," but "having charming manners, he was soon the intimate of a number of men with long and expensive habits." A more disciplined childhood and some kind of impression about his responsibilities as a representative of his class might have made a difference in his attitude. Even so, sometimes "blood will out." In THE BERYL CORONET, Arthur Holder ultimately came through admirably in a pinch.

Many a parent's fondest hopes for the future have been deflated by a son such as James McCarthy. He was "not a very quick-witted youth, though comely to look at, and I should think, sound at heart." Despite failings that surely were apparent to his father, there was still a prospect for a suitable marriage, but those plans were thwarted by James' decision to elope with a local barmaid. This led inevitably to loud arguments and hard feelings within the McCarthy family, and ultimately to a charge of murder against the feckless (but innocent) James. Like Arthur Holder, he was eventually cleared of wrongdoing, thanks to Holmes' investigation of THE BOSCOMBE VALLEY MYSTERY. One can imagine James regaling his wife and her besotted customers at the local inn with his version of the tale for many years to come.

Finally, though well-meaning enough and far more worthy in a personal sense than the others just mentioned, John Openshaw of THE FIVE ORANGE PIPS was the unfortunate choice of fate to be the last in his family line. Watson wrote that "he was young, some two-and-twenty on the outside, well-groomed and trimly clad, with something of refinement and delicacy in his bearing." One would have hoped that he would turn to Sherlock Holmes long before he did (especially after two murders). And one would also hope that someone fully armed and cognizant of his personal danger would not be waylaid and murdered without even a sign of struggle, but in young Openshaw's case, those hopes would be dashed.

A family relation need not be young, however, to be either a trial or a disappointment for the other members of his clan, as the characters of *The Case-Book of Sherlock Holmes*—three fathers and a parasitic brother—demonstrate. Age does not always produce good judgment, good manners, or good behavior. Sometimes, bad habits or bad characteristics are simply magnified in later years. These four individuals fairly begged to be knocked off their high horses, and Holmes was just the man to do it.

There is reason to wonder how Tom Bellamy of THE LION'S MANE could be the father of both the lovely and admirable Maud and her churlish brother. Bellamy was "a middle-aged man with a flaming red beard. He seemed to be in an angry mood, and his face as florid as his hair." Bellamy appeared to be something of a tyrant, and there are hints that he demanded absolute obedience and control in his own household.

Perhaps he did not have much authority anywhere else. In any event, Maud herself complained that her father was guilty of prejudice and that he never showed her any sympathy

Colonel Emsworth of THE BLANCHED SOLDIER was a military man, and he also was disposed toward petty household tyranny. As an officer, he undoubtedly was accustomed to being instantly obeyed and rarely challenged. James M. Dodd described Colonel Emsworth as "a hard nail" and "the greatest martinet in the Army in his day . . . a curmudgeon." Furthermore, we are told that "the old man was sometimes a bully . . . a huge, bow-backed man with a smoky skin and a straggling gray beard." His fierceness and his almost insufferable rudeness might be explained by his paternal instincts, his desire to protect his son; but it seems likely that life in the Emsworth home was usually far from pleasant.

Another military man, the celebrated General de Merville, took exactly the opposite course in THE ILLUSTRIOUS CLIENT. He must have been a more tender-hearted fellow, perhaps because he wanted to protect a daughter rather than a son. Holmes gave a sad description of him: "De Merville is a broken man. The strong soldier has been utterly demoralized . . . He has lost the nerve which never failed him on the battlefield and has become a weak, doddering old man." If Bellamy and Emsworth asserted themselves too much, de Merville asserted himself too little. One has to wonder how Colonel Emsworth, the celebrated man of action, would have handled Baron Gruner and how the compassionate General de Merville would have dealt with Godfrey Emsworth's unfortunate condition.

Finally, the worthless spendthrift brother, the bane of many a modern family, also existed in the time of Sherlock Holmes. Sir Robert Norberton had nothing of his own and depended on his sister, the "old lady," for his upkeep in SHOSCOMBE OLD PLACE. Probably in his fifties or early sixties, "he was a terrible figure, huge in stature and fierce in manner." This was all for show; in reality he was something of a humbug. Irresponsible in his gambling (reminding one of young Arthur Holder in THE BERYL CORONET), and searching for a way out, he did take action. Characteristically, however, he did so in a fundamentally dishonest way. Age is no protection against either poor judgment or a lack of ethics.

Specialists

Four young men in *The Adventures of Sherlock Holmes* were engaged in trades of one kind or another. They would be considered blue-collar workers in today's society. All were making their way in the world, only one of them in a completely honest way, in the commercial system of the time. Like millions of others, they were men with an occupation, a specialty of some sort that put them into the working middle class that made the English economy so strong and the empire so powerful.

The rogue of this group, of course, was John Clay "the murderer, thief, smasher and forger" who nevertheless posed as a clerk in a pawn shop in THE RED-HEADED LEAGUE and earned some measure of respect from Sherlock Holmes. "He's a young man," said Holmes, "but he is at the head of his profession. He's a remarkable man, is young John Clay. His brain is as cunning as his fingers." By "his profession," Holmes meant the criminal profession, not clerking, but there is no doubt that Clay was considered an "up and comer" by his associates as well as his adversaries.

For sheer chutzpah, Clay might have met his match with Neville St. Clair, central figure in THE MAN WITH THE TWISTED LIP, a former newspaper reporter who earned a gentleman's income disguised as a pitiful beggar. From all appearances, the 37-year-old St. Clair was a model citizen: "a man of temperate habits, a good husband, a very affectionate father, and a man who is popular with all who know him." If you can put aside defrauding the public, deceiving his wife, and hanging around opium dens, what more could anyone ask of him?

Then there is the 26-year-old plumber, John Horner, a man of "intense emotion" who had his own run-ins with the law, including "a previous conviction for robbery." When arrested (falsely this time) for stealing a famous gem from a guest at the Hotel Cosmopolitan in THE BLUE CARBUNCLE, this vigorous young man "struggled frantically and protested his innocence in the strongest terms." One can only hope that he regained his job after this incident, but attitudes being what they were at the time, that hope is probably a vain one.

Victor Hatherley was a hydraulic engineer, a man who could tinker with complicated machinery and get it back in working order, even in the middle of the night. Watson described him succinctly: "He was young, not more than five-and-twenty, I should say, with a strong, masculine face." In other words, he was another fine young product of British stock of the stiff-upper-lip variety. But Hatherly was also something of a Superman. Remember, in THE ENGINEER'S THUMB, he lost his thumb "torn right out from the roots" after an attempt on his life, wrapped it in a handkerchief, and had it stitched up with no more anesthesia than brandy and water. And despite his all-night ordeal, nothing would do but that he eat a hearty breakfast, unburden himself to Sherlock Holmes, and return to the scene of the crime before taking any sort of a rest. What a man!

Contrast these young men of the trades, then, to the aged men of the aristocracy and the professions mentioned in *The Case-Book of Sherlock Holmes*. These doddering old fellows may have been strapping and vigorous in their youth, but all of them had succumbed to the frailties of old age. Despite good intentions and positions of prominence and influence, they were not the sort to inspire much in the way of confidence. They were more sluggish than forceful, more associated with lethargy than vitality.

Nathan Garrideb, age 60-plus, was the very picture of a man who had let himself go. "He had a cadaverous face, with the dull dead skin of a man to whom exercise was unknown. Large round spectacles and a small projecting goat's beard combined with this stooping attitude." Educated and eccentric with a "thin, quavering voice," he recognized his limitations and described himself as "not too strong." As detailed in THE THREE GARRIDEBS, his desire for money was not based so much on greed as in his zeal for collecting and scientific research, but he was doomed to disappointment and a return to this generally unhealthy lifestyle.

Another unimpressive professional was the otherwise "capable" lawyer, Mr. Sutro of THE THREE GABLES, who was willing to give Mary Maberley advice from the comfort of his armchair, but could not find the time to be on hand when a house agent called to get her to sign a life-changing legal agreement. Sherlock Holmes hoped that Sutro—a "gray old gentleman"—could provide Mrs. Maberley some degree of protection. But Holmes was disappointed, and said so: "I made a mistake, I fear . . . This fellow has clearly proved a broken reed."

Lord Cantlemere, an "old peer" who had served "fifty years of official life" was another shell of his former self who was no more adept at requesting help than providing it. In THE MAZARIN STONE, he was depicted as "a thin, austere figure with a hatchet face and drooping mid-Victorian whiskers of a glossy blackness which hardly corresponded with the rounded shoulders and feeble gait." Billy the page considered Cantlemere to be "a stiff'un," and Watson commented on his "sallow cheeks," while Holmes himself could not resist taunting the old man.

Finally, there was Robert Ferguson, Watson's old friend and athletic rival, who became the senior partner in a tea brokering firm. Ferguson, who brought THE SUSSEX VAMPIRE case to the attention of Sherlock Holmes, was not as Watson remembered him: "There is surely nothing in life more painful than to meet the wreck of a fine athlete whom one has known in his prime. His great frame had fallen, his flaxen hair was scanty, and his shoulders were bowed." The pain that Watson felt, however, was not just for the "good-natured" Ferguson—"I fear that I roused corresponding emotions in him." Watson first knew Ferguson as a strong and skillful athlete, but he left him "choking" and "quivering" with grief.

Conclusion

"You don't look quite the man you did."

With that comment to Watson, Ferguson may have provided some insight not just about his old rival on the field, but also about what Conan Doyle was feeling about himself by the time *The Case-Book of Sherlock Holmes* was being written.

Sherlock Holmes had come to some fatalistic conclusions about life toward the end of his career. "But is not all life pathetic and futile?" he asked. "We reach. We grasp. And what is left in our hands at the end? A shadow. Or worse than a shadow—misery." Thankfully, that was an uncharacteristically pessimistic view of the world for Holmes, Watson or Conan Doyle. But in some ways it denotes the common theme of the old men of *The Case-Book*. As a group, they had lost the confidence and optimism possessed by the younger men of *The Adventures*, both good and bad. These common threads, running through two sets of stories separated by many years in their composition and in their occurrence, perhaps are to be expected, a natural adjustment for authors or doctors or detectives—or for any one of us.

Trailblazers in the World of Ideas

Sherlock Holmes and the Poets Laureate

Early in the association of Sherlock Holmes and Dr. John H. Watson, the good doctor decided to put together his now-famous, and often completely erroneous, catalogue of the "limits" of Sherlock Holmes. The very first item on Watson's list, as recorded in *A Study in Scarlet* was: "1. Knowledge of Literature.—Nil."

Over the years, Watson would have good reason to question his first impressions of Holmes. Certainly, a listing of his friend's abilities only a short time later would have produced a much different result. Holmes was much more knowledgeable about a wide range of subjects than Watson could have realized.

A Quotation from Horace

Watson may have altered his ideas about Holmes and literature before the end of their first case together. At the conclusion of *A Study in Scarlet*, Lestrade and Gregson were given all the credit in *The Echo* for the apprehension of Jefferson Hope. Sherlock Holmes was provided with nothing more than a condescending nod in that newspaper—a pattern which would be repeated many times in the course of his career.

Holmes simply laughed at the newspaper account, but Watson promised to tell the whole story to the public, saying, "In the meantime you must make yourself contented by the consciousness of success, like the Roman miser—

Populus me sibilat, at mihi plaudo
Ipse domi simul ac nummos contemplar in arca."

Which, translated, means, "People hiss at me, but I am satisfied with myself; I stay at home and contemplate the money in my strong-box." This quotation is from Horace's *First Book of Satires* (I:66-67), which appeared in 35 BC. Watson's willingness to use a couple of lines from classical literature—and to use the original Latin—indicates that he had come to an understanding about Holmes' knowledge of literature that was far different than what he had written on the list he constructed only a short time earlier. Surely he would not have quoted Latin to someone if he truly believed that his familiarity with literature was "nil."

Beyond that, however, is Watson's fundamental misunderstanding of Sherlock Holmes and what motivated him—a misconception revealed plainly by the good doctor's use of this quotation. Watson was assuming that Holmes would be satisfied, at least temporarily, without public credit, but with a financial reward for this efforts in the capture of Jefferson Hope. We know from numerous canonical references that the problem itself, not the fee, was Holmes' primary interest. But Watson did not possess that kind of awareness in this, his first case with Holmes.

Ultimately, Dr. Watson can be forgiven for this inappropriate citation from Horace. Perhaps, though, Holmes was a bit insulted or irritated by the quotation at the time. Certainly, he ignored it for the moment. But he didn't forget. And by the end of A CASE OF IDENTITY, he had a chance to toss it back at Watson a little by alluding to Hafiz, a lyric poet of 14th Century Persia who was just as significant to his era as was Horace to ancient Rome. "There is as much sense in Hafiz as in Horace, and as much knowledge of the world," Holmes commented. This was a two-birds-with-one-stone line for Holmes: In addition to debunking Watson's erroneous assumptions about his work, he was also demolishing once and for all that "Knowledge of Literature.—Nil" nonsense.

As the years went by, Watson came to a better understanding of his brilliant friend. He recognized in THE NOBLE BACHELOR that Holmes worked "rather for the love of his art than for the acquirement of wealth." In a more expansive description of Holmes' true way of thinking in BLACK PETER, Watson noted: "So unworldly was he—or so capricious—that he frequently refused his help to the powerful or wealthy where the problem made no appeal to his sympathies, while he would devote weeks of most intense application to the affairs of some humble client whose case presented those strange and dramatic qualities which appealed to his imagination and challenged his ingenuity."

Later in life, that inappropriate and perhaps offensive quotation from Horace would never enter Watson's thoughts, at least as they related to

Holmes. Surely, he looked back at his closing lines in *A Study in Scarlet* with a touch of discomfort or even embarrassment.

Horace as Role Model

Ironically, considering Watson's *faux pas*, Horace would have a great appeal for a man such as Sherlock Holmes. Classical scholar William S. Anderson made the following pertinent observation: "As a lyricist, Horace is unique among Roman poets and rare among world writers in speaking with a voice of reason that is utterly controlled. He . . . calls for temperate pleasures, rejecting both extravagant passion and totally dispassionate, impersonal preoccupation with monetary matters."

Consider, as well, another informed evaluation of the ancient Roman poet. "Horace was Epicurean in his rationalism and his enjoyment of friendship and quiet pleasures, Stoic in his conviction of the importance of morality and public duty, and Peripatetic in his pursuit of the golden mean," states L.P. Wilkinson. A thorough understanding of otherwise arcane philosophies is not really necessary for the sake of a generalized comparison, which (if not taken too far) can be interesting.

In many ways, such descriptions fit Sherlock Holmes almost perfectly, and they help bring Horace into focus as a role model that Sherlock Holmes might very well have wanted to emulate. Certainly, he enjoyed his "friendship" with Watson; his "pleasures," such as smoking or music, were both temperate and quiet; his lack of emphasis on "monetary matters" was well-established; his "morality" was self-developed, but continually evident; and his choice of professions and his work on the side of the law revealed a sense of "public duty."

The study of Horace and other classical writers was considered part of any well-educated Victorian's academic background. So much so, in fact, that Dr. Thorneycroft Huxtable thought it likely that his book on the Roman poet would be sufficiently well-known to serve as an introduction. "*Huxtable's Sidelights on Horace* may probably recall my name to your memories," he told Holmes and Watson in THE PRIORY SCHOOL. Perhaps that statement contained a bit of hubris, reflecting the tunnel vision of a specialist or enthusiast. Even so, an idea either that "the founder and principal" of the "best and most select preparatory school in England" was also an expert on Horace or that his book on the subject might have been widely-known would not necessarily be far-fetched. Such credentials would have been expected from the leader of such an institution, and such a book may have been required reading for students of the time.

Horace—Quintus Horatius Flaccus (65-8 BC)—was born in Southern Italy and has to be considered one of the great survivors of ancient politics. Educated in Rome and Athens, he served in the Republican army under Brutus and returned to Rome after being on the losing side of the Battle of Philippi. Using his friendship with the epic poet Virgil, who wrote *The Aeneid*, Horace wound up working as a bureaucrat in the government of Brutus' victorious enemy, Octavian. The nephew and heir of Julius Caesar, Octavian preferred the name Augustus and became the first Roman emperor.

Horace was a literary pioneer, and he knew it. His goal was to create Roman lyric poetry that could stand beside the Greek, and today he is considered the poet laureate of the Augustan Age. It helped that Augustus liked him, despite Horace having fought for one of the men who stabbed his Uncle Julius. In fact, Horace became part of what might have been considered the emperor's "Rat Pack", had there been such a notion at the time—and he got to play Caesar's Palace, literally. The poet did not look anything like Holmes—Horace was "short and fat," and Augustus teased him about it. But Holmes was an admirer of ideas. Horace's life was interesting, his work was quotable, and his literary influence was long-lasting.

So three separate references to Horace in the Sherlockian saga—Watson's quotation in *A Study in Scarlet*, Holmes' belated retort in A CASE OF IDENTITY and Huxtable's citation in THE PRIORY SCHOOL—are not really unusual. However, there is another literary allusion in the canon which, when considered with these mentions of Horace, suggests that Sherlock Holmes was well-acquainted with his work, considered him worthy of emulation, and placed himself on the same level as an innovator in his chosen field.

A Pocket Full of Petrarch

Watson provides a bit of illumination concerning the well-read Sherlock Holmes in THE BOSCOMBE VALLEY MYSTERY as they relaxed while riding in a railway car between London and the "pretty little country-town of Ross" in Herefordshire. Says Holmes, "And now here is my pocket Petrarch, and not another word shall I say of this case until we are on the scene of the action."

Petrarch—Francesco Petrarca (1304-1374)—was, like Horace, a literary pioneer. In this case, he was a major force in the development of the Renaissance. He liked to write poems about a girl named Laura, although no one knows for sure if she was a real person or not. Just as

Horace was a friend of Virgil, Petrarch had a famous writer friend by the name of Giovanni Boccaccio, the author of *The Decameron*. Petrarch was something of a survivor himself. His father got kicked out of Florence by a new and intolerant regime, and Petrarch went with him. He studied at Montpellier (although it is unlikely he was studying coal tar derivatives there, as did Sherlock Holmes) and then moved on to Bologna, where he studied law.

What Petrarch really enjoyed, however, was writing and Latin literature. He spent a good amount of his time roaming around Europe—France, Germany, Italy and Spain, among other, lesser-known countries, of which there were many in 14th Century Europe—searching for old Latin classics and manuscripts. In 1347, he bought a copy of the works of Horace, and there is "a marked Horatian influence in some of his poems." Like Horace, Petrarch was crowned as a poet laureate in Rome, and he spent most of his later years moving from place to place and making a living from his international celebrity. If he were alive today, he might be found in O.J.'s guest house. But, by and large, he was probably the greatest scholar of his age, and he managed to mix his interests in classical culture and Christianity in a way that influenced Western thought tremendously. He is one of those figures most people never even heard of, but who had a lot to do with our cultural groundings.

Sherlock Holmes must have admired Petrarch in many ways. That he would carry a pocket edition of his poetry is proof enough of that, of course. But Petrarch was similar to Holmes in another way. Both of them acquired knowledge in a non-systematic multi-disciplinary manner. For Petrarch, religion, law, literature, ancient history, diplomacy, manuscript-hunting, ethics and linguistics all were subjects he pursued as he developed his world view. Young Stamford summed up Holmes' method of learning in *A Study in Scarlet*: "His studies are very desultory and eccentric, but he has amassed a lot of out-of-the-way knowledge which would astonish his professors." One of the interests that Holmes and Petrarch shared was the work of that ancient Roman poet—Horace.

Poets and Pioneers

Holmes was not a poet. Nor, judging by the two adventures he wrote himself, was he a particularly great writer. Yet, he was well-read, literate in the truest sense of the word, and an admirer of two of the greatest poets of Western literature, Horace and Petrarch.

Every Sherlockian has quoted the famous line from A SCANDAL IN BOHEMIA that Holmes made about Dr. Watson: "I am lost without my

Boswell." The reference, of course is to James Boswell, whose *Life of Samuel Johnson*, published seven years after Johnson's death, is generally considered to be the greatest biography ever written. There is some thought that Boswell's fawning idol-worship (similar to Watson's generally uncritical adoration of Holmes), ironically, may have damaged Johnson's personal credibility and reputation as a writer.

Be that as it may, if Holmes looked at Watson as a Boswell, then he must have looked upon himself as a Samuel Johnson, another literary pioneer whose *A Dictionary of the English Language* was original and remained unrivaled until the appearance of the *Oxford English Dictionary* in the 1880s. Hopefully, Holmes did not carry the Watson-Boswell comparison to an extreme. Both of them possessed a self-image as something of a ladies' man, but Boswell was a sexual addict who liked prostitutes and managed to contract gonorrhea 17 times over a period of 30 years. Watson seems to have approached women with a more romantic, idealistic and less proactive way—more likely to marry a woman for sex rather than to pay one for it.

Johnson was also familiar with Horace, and he quoted the Roman poet many times in various writings, but not enough to make him a Horatian devotee such as either Petrarch or Thorneycroft Huxtable. The significance of the Boswell reference was to once again reaffirm Holmes' knowledge of literature and of literary figures, and to identify him—in his own mind and in the minds of those who read his adventures—as a pioneer in the mold of Horace, Petrarch or even Johnson.

These men were trailblazers in the world of ideas. Horace was the first to make lyric poetry written in Latin as important as that written in Greek. Petrarch was the first to combine classic themes with Western thought. Johnson was the first to put together an English language dictionary. And Sherlock Holmes was the first in his chosen field: "Well, I have a trade of my own. I suppose I am the only one in the world. I'm a consulting detective," he told Watson in *A Study in Scarlet*.

Holmes' knowledge of literary figures such as Horace, Hafiz, Petrarch, Johnson and Boswell, Shakespeare and others is demonstrated throughout the Sherlockian tales. Perhaps he chose his reading material not just for the quality of the writing or the insights into human nature he might have gleaned, but also because he identified with the authors, and rightly so. We do know that Sherlock Holmes chose all of his intellectual pursuits very carefully. "Depend upon it there comes a time when for every addition of knowledge you forget something that you knew before," he said. "It is of the highest importance, therefore, not to have useless facts elbowing out the useful ones." Sherlock Holmes, who permitted no information without an obvious value to him to occupy his mind, admired these authors and studied them. That alone is a powerful recommendation for their works, and an equally powerful incentive to read them for ourselves.

My Arrangement with Mr. Holmes

by Mrs. Neville St. Clair

"Come along, Neville."

"Dearest, are you sure about this? Perhaps we should consider our position a little more carefully."

I sighed. My husband and I had just dismissed our cab, and we were standing at the door of 221B Baker Street.

"Neville, we have discussed this quite enough." I knew as I spoke how sharp I sounded, but sharpness—once so foreign to my nature—had become a frequent visitor to my conversations of the past week. "We have no choice about seeing Mr. Holmes. After all, he earned his fee, and we must deliver it. As for the other . . . Well, I have no intention of debating it with you any further."

With that, I rang the bell, and Neville said no more. My summons was answered by a middle-aged woman, no doubt the landlady; but before I could even ask for Mr. Holmes, I heard his voice from a door at the top of the stairs.

"It's all right, Mrs. Hudson," he called to her. "Mr. and Mrs. St. Clair are more than welcome. Please come up, by all means, both of you."

We climbed the steps and entered the apartment. Neville clutched his hat tightly and looked mostly at the floor, but he finally had the presence of mind to shake hands with Mr. Holmes as I glanced around the lodgings. Something in my expression must have revealed my thoughts to the detective.

"I am afraid that the clutter of a bachelor, especially one with such unusual preoccupations, might offend the sensibilities of a lady like yourself, Mrs. St. Clair," he said with a smile. "But, here, let me offer you a seat. You remember my friend and associate, Dr. Watson?"

"Of course." Dr. Watson was standing near the hearth with a puzzled look upon his face. "I hope you are well, doctor."

"Well? Yes, well, yes I am. Thank you. And you?" Dr. Watson was quite uncomfortable, but his fumbling had the effect of strengthening my own resolve. I laughed, then laughed again at the startled look upon his face. "We are very well, thank you." I seated myself comfortably on a cushioned chair with arms, while Neville sat slightly behind me, very erect and still gripping his hat.

"May I offer you some tea?" Holmes asked. "Mrs. Hudson can bring up a tray directly." When I declined for both of us, he proceeded to fill his pipe with tobacco which he apparently kept in a Persian slipper. I found that quite disgusting, but of course made no comment. "I am pleased to see you both, although I know that you, Mr. St. Clair, not only did not wish to come but suggested quite a few reasons to avoid this visit."

"But how could you know that?" Neville's voice was almost a squeak. I looked at him with more than a little irritation, and he fidgeted nervously in his chair.

"I was watching you from my window," Holmes explained. "Although I could not hear your conversation at our doorstep, it was not particularly difficult to understand the general direction it was taking. Clearly, you were making a final appeal to your wife. A first objection would have produced more discussion, but she cut you off quickly. And your anxiety since your arrival certainly confirms my suspicions. On the other hand, Mrs. St. Clair, you seem to have a definite purpose in mind."

"Indeed I do, Mr. Holmes," I replied. For one thing, there is the matter of your fee. I engaged you to find out what happened to my husband, and you did just that. There is no question about your results, even if I must fault your methods." With this comment, I reached into my handbag and produced an envelope, which I offered to Mr. Holmes, who had settled into his armchair. He took it from me, opened it, and said nothing. Only the slight arching of one eyebrow revealed anything of his thoughts as he passed the cheque to Dr. Watson, who was not so reserved.

"Oh, my!" Dr. Watson exclaimed with clear surprise. "That is quite generous, Mrs. St. Clair!"

"Quite so," added Holmes. "In fact, it is twice the fee we discussed. But before we deal with this matter of payment, I must ask you to explain your remark about my methods. What exactly did you mean by that?"

Both Holmes and Watson addressed their comments directly to me. Neville's evident desire to disappear was actually succeeding to a certain degree. He said nothing and remained motionless; even his breathing was restrained.

"I mean the dramatic face washing in Neville's Bow Street cell. I mean his exposure in front of Inspector Bradstreet and Dr. Watson. I engaged you to find out what happened to my husband and to locate him or his dead body, not to humiliate him." I was speaking with some heat, but Holmes listened impassively. "The final denouement of your investigation might have been dramatic and self-satisfying, but it was unnecessary to put Neville through such an episode."

Holmes appeared to be turning this over in him mind, but Dr. Watson was clearly incensed and his face was quite red.

"My dear Mrs. St. Clair, you seem to forget that your husband was using an alias and a disguise while being held under suspicion of murder," he objected with some fervor. "Not only that, the resources of Scotland Yard, not to mention those of Sherlock Holmes, were being expended in a search for your husband. Mr. Neville St. Clair spent years perpetuating his fraud, pretending to be a crippled beggar, on the public streets of London. You were beside yourself with worry and fear, and the possible effect on your two children can only be imagined. I certainly cannot agree that *he* has been wronged in this affair." With this final comment, Dr. Watson extended his arm to point at Neville, who cringed and sank father into his chair.

I glared at the doctor. Before I could respond, however, Holmes intervened. "That's all right, Watson. But Mrs. St. Clair, how exactly do you think I should have proceeded?"

"You had my husband's letter to me, Mr. Holmes, and you had your suspicions. You were in my own home with both. We had discussed the case the previous evening. I told you at that time that I was not hysterical nor given to fainting, and your own observations, as acute as they are, must have confirmed that judgment of my character. You had no qualms about telling me you thought Neville was dead. Why did you hesitate to tell me you thought he was alive?"

The three men in that room stared at me in silence. Holmes was concentrating on every word I said. Watson seemed stunned. I knew Neville was in anguish, but he dared not say a word.

"I was your client, not Scotland Yard," I continued. "You should have shared your theory with me. With Neville's letter in hand, with a slight change in my recollections of that afternoon on Swandam Lane, with your assurances, we could have freed the man known as Hugh Boone from his cell. There was, after all, no real evidence against him, and the letter provided real evidence of his innocence. A whispered word would have convinced him to leave Bow Street quietly with us. The confrontation, the exposure of Neville's true occupation, the unavoidable embarrassment and shame, could have been revealed here in these rooms or even at the Cedars, in the privacy of our own home. No, Mr. Holmes, there was no need for your theatrics that morning."

Watson started once again to speak, but Holmes hushed him with a simple gesture. I had made my case, and I relaxed a little as he sat considering my comments and smoking his pipe. Only the ticking of a clock disturbed the stillness of those rooms.

"I am not accustomed to explaining my methods, Mrs. St. Clair," he said finally. "I pursue problems that interest me. The fee is incidental. As I recall, you were quite desperate for assistance and placed no conditions on my services. I would not have accepted your conditions in any event. So I will make no apology to you for the way I exposed the truth of this matter. However, I must concede that there is some merit in what you have said. Knowing as I now do what your feelings are, if I could change what has occurred, I would. But I cannot. So where does that leave us?"

This was not exactly what I had expected. Now, it was my turn to consider. Dr. Watson evidently was beyond understanding either the situation or his friend's attitude. I suspected that even this remote approximation of an apology was unusual for Sherlock Holmes, and his friend was taken aback by it. Watson let his eyes roam about the room as if he were searching for something. My husband remained motionless. Holmes and I regarded each other speculatively, and neither of us lowered our eyes. After a short reflection, I determined that this particular subject was exhausted. Holmes was right; the past cannot be changed, and neither the payment of the fee nor this dispute about the revelation of Neville's secret identity was my main purpose in coming to Baker Street anyway.

I broke the silence. "Very well, Mr. Holmes, I have aired my complaint. Perhaps that is enough. In any event, my real business here has not yet been addressed."

"Indeed?" Holmes allowed himself a look of mild surprise. "What, then, is your real business, as you put it?"

I had been seated long enough, so I arose from my chair, took a breath, and glanced idly at the clutter of the mantle as I gathered my thoughts. I could not help but notice that Holmes kept letters transfixed to the wall with a knife. I remember thinking that he was certainly a queer sort of fellow, but someone once told me that all men of genius give themselves license to pursue their eccentricities.

"Mr. Holmes, Dr. Watson, you have both been guests in our home. What did you think of it?"

"It is certainly lovely in every respect," Watson replied after a brief pause. This was quite a change in the direction of our discussion, and his tone and attitude changed with it. "The grounds are well kept; it is decorated with impeccable taste; it is spacious and comfortable. The servants are efficient and well-mannered. I thought at the time that it was the sort of home in the country that most of us hope to enjoy, but few of us actually attain."

"Would you say, Dr. Watson, that the Cedars is suitable for rearing two children?"

"Without a doubt."

I nodded. "You are correct. The Cedars is a lovely place, and we have been extremely happy there. You might say we have had a charmed existence. I am a brewer's daughter, and Neville is the son of a school-master. We come from modest but respectable backgrounds, and neither of us had any reason to expect more than the same modest but respectable lifestyle of our rearing. I have considered myself fortunate to have a husband who was given neither to drink nor to violence, who showed great affection always to me and to our children, and who is popular with all who know him. That he was so successful financially was more than I could have hoped, and we have used his income responsibly and well."

"But his financial success, as you call it, was based on a deception." Through some unspoken agreement, Dr. Watson had taken up the conversation. I stood in front of the fireplace with my hands clasped before me, as if I were on a small stage. But I was suffering from no stage fright. I enjoyed the undivided attention of Watson and Neville. Sherlock Holmes had finished his pipe, and he appeared to be almost asleep, but I knew he was taking in every word. I ignored Dr. Watson's observation and continued.

"Two weeks ago, however, our lives were altered when I saw Neville at the window of that horrible and filthy place. My fears for his safety turned first to the horror of what he had been doing, then to an irrational denial of the facts, then to anger . . ."

"Yes, much anger." Neville finally spoke, this time not with a squeak, but with a note of sadness and resignation. I smiled at the thought of the many long hours he had endured with my tears, accusations and complaints. Poor Neville. I expect there were many times over the past week he would rather have been back in that cell in Bow Street than listening to me.

" . . . then to anger, and then at last to acceptance. I know I seem small and soft and very feminine to you gentlemen, and perhaps you have a low opinion of my sex." At this, I noticed that Watson glanced meaningfully at Holmes, but the detective did not move as much as an eyelid. "But there is resolution in me as well. I have come to accept what my husband has been doing, what choice do I have? But I have come to a decision as well, and Neville has—reluctantly I must say—concurred with that decision."

I paused. After a moment, Watson asked the obvious question. "And what decision might that be?"

"We have no intention of giving up what we have acquired, Dr. Watson. My husband has been earning 700 pounds a year in his role as the beggar Hugh Boone. That's a gentleman's income. We have a wonderful home, a respectable lifestyle, and the future of two children to consider. For him to return to reporting for a newspaper or even to the stage might satisfy the moral standards of our time, but it will not put one loaf of bread on our table. We will not willingly surrender the Cedars, nor will we be forced out of our position in Kent. Neville broke no laws, and there is no reason he cannot return to his successful trade of selling wax vestas on Threadneedle Street." I held my chin high as I made this announcement, and I spoke with what I hoped would be an air of defiance and authority. I was proud that my voice did not shake or crack.

Watson, however, was nearly purple with his outrage and he was fairly sputtering by the time I had concluded this little speech. "Surely, you cannot be serious! After what has already transpired, how can you hope to continue such a deception?"

With firmness, I answered all of the objections he raised. I was well-prepared, since Neville and I had gone over every one of them, and several others, many times. Neville's solemn promise to Inspector Bradstreet that there would be no more of Hugh Boone would be kept as a matter of necessity. He was known to the police in that character, so it was useless to continue using it. Neville had proved himself more than capable of transforming himself into a convincing and pitiable cripple, and we were already working on a new disguise that would be just as compelling.

As for the lascar, he had been well-paid for many years, and he would welcome the opportunity to continue providing a safe haven for Neville's operations. He already knew that Hugh Boone had been released for a lack of evidence, and Inspector Bradstreet had assured us of his intention to keep his knowledge about Neville a secret. The lascar would understand Neville's desire to change his disguise now that Boone had come under such close police scrutiny. The old room above the opium den would be made available as it had been for many years, although probably at an increased cost.

"But what of the shame of such a course of action, Mrs. St. Clair?" Watson asked after all of his practical objections had been defeated. "Your husband agonized over the possibility of a family blot, a stain upon his children, the ruination of his reputation. What of his fear of exposure, which might come at any time?"

"This was the most difficult question for us to answer, but we have resolved it to our satisfaction," I replied. "I have chosen to view Neville's begging in disguise as nothing more than being paid for his acting ability. What he receives is freely given, and what he gives is a sense of satisfaction that his benefactor has done some good in the world. As for a blot on our honor, there would be many questions about our sudden loss of home and station—questions which could not be answered, and since they cannot be answered will be the subject of damaging speculation and rumor. By taking the course we have chosen, we believe we actually have a better chance of keeping our reputation. As for discovery, Neville kept Hugh Boone alive for many years without being discovered, and I am confident he can do the same with his new beggar as well."

Watson, sank back into his chair as I resumed my seat. "There is nothing more I can say, Mrs. St. Clair, except to tell you that I am disappointed. I had, until today, considered you to be a respectable lady and an innocent victim of your husband's deceptions, and I am sorry to see you become his accomplice."

Except to pack and smoke another pipe, Sherlock Holmes had done nothing throughout this exchange, but he roused himself as Watson was speaking and stood in the place I had just occupied.

"I make no such moral judgments, Mrs. St. Clair, although I am sure you will never convince such a solid citizen as Dr. Watson," he said. "What your husband does for a living is really no concern of mine. I have found this entire episode to be a fascinating experience. However, I must question the need for this visit at all. The fee could have been delivered by messenger, and your husband could have resumed his chosen profession, with your aid and blessing and in a new costume, at any time. Why do you find it necessary to advise me of your intentions?"

"Because, Mr. Holmes, I have learned enough from my association with you to know that our secret would not go undetected as long as you are in London. Oh, we can deceive Inspector Bradstreet and his colleagues easily enough, but you could be a problem for us. You knew of Hugh Boone as a professional beggar for years, and you said yourself that you occasionally visit the Bar of Gold in Upper Swandam Lane in a disguise of your own. I have no illusions about your abilities, and I know that you would see through Neville's new identity quickly enough." I could tell he was pleased by this explanation. I did not mean it as flattery, but I knew that I had touched on the man's vanity.

"And you have come, not to appeal to my discretion, but to make an agreement, have you not?" Holmes was smiling, and I returned his smile.

At this moment, I was sure that we were going to come to a mutually beneficial arrangement.

"I thought you would understand, Mr. Holmes. Of course, Neville hears and sees a great deal in his disguise—and some of it could be of great use to you in your investigations. A system of communication through one of your famous Baker Street Irregulars could be arranged easily enough, and you can always send a letter or telegram directly to the Cedars. He will keep his eyes and ears open and provide you with whatever information you might require. And knowing that we are assisting with your investigations adds justification to our decision."

Watson was much agitated once again. "Holmes, you are not going to join in this conspiracy as well, are you?"

"I am a confidential consultant, Watson. I would not reveal Mr. St. Clair's identity under any circumstances, but the idea of having such a reliable informant at my disposal certainly appeals to me. Clearly, the St. Clairs have made their decision, and I see little likelihood that they will change their minds. I would be foolish not to take advantage of the offer." Watson harrumphed, but said nothing, so Holmes continued. "But I have not heard from the principal character in this case. Mr. St. Clair, your wife has done all the talking. Can we assume that you are in full agreement?"

Neville appeared to be startled by the question, but he recovered quickly enough. "Yes." Then more strongly, "Yes, Mr. Holmes. I want to continue to provide a good home for my family, to live as we have grown accustomed to living, to enjoy the financial security my unusual trade has brought to us. The arrangement my wife has described is agreeable to me."

"Then it is settled. I will be looking for you in your old place and in your new disguise."

Our business was completed, so we made our way to the door. But before we left, Neville turned to Sherlock Holmes with one last comment.

"You were right, you know, Mr. Holmes."

"How is that?"

"You were right in what you said to me in that cell in Bow Street."

"You must refresh my memory. Much was said that morning."

"You said, and these were your exact words, 'You would have done better to have trusted your wife'."

Holmes smiled and clapped Neville on the back, and we were on or way.

Sightings at Twilight

That guy? Now there's a real geek. I mean, what kind of a weirdo spends his time working out math problems on a blackboard? I've seen him through his window. And sometimes, he'll sit hunched over his desk for hours at a time, like some kind of a spider waiting for a bug. No wonder his posture is so bad. Never gets any sun either—just a tall, skinny, gloomy, pale old man. The computer nerds have got nothing on him!

And that tic! The guy can't seem to hold his head still. It's really kind of gross—like a snake, or a jack-in-the-box bouncing around, or one of those guys from *A Night at the Roxbury*. Gives you the creeps.

Check out that face and those clothes. His eyes are all sunk in his head; but they're puckered, like he's squinting at you to get a better look. And he's always wearing that long coat. How strange is that? If you ask me, he's the most likely guy in town to be hanging around a playground.

Yeah, the light-bulb head doesn't help any. If he tried, he could have gotten that part in *Young Frankenstein*, or maybe he could have been Lurch. He'd be right at home with the Addams Family.

I heard he's some kind of college professor, or used to be. The "nutty professor" is more like it. He lost his job, though—only works part-time at the Army base, tutoring the officer candidates in math. That dopey doctor over in the next street told me about it. Oh, you know, the one who only works about half the time because he's always running off with some friend of his. Boy, his wife just *stays* mad.

Anyway, this professor, like I said, he lost his job. All the doctor would say about it is something about "dark rumors." Another one of those things he says the world is not yet ready to hear. That goofball has a lot of those. I think he's full of it.

Dark rumors? Sounds like some kind of a pervert to me. You won't catch me hanging around the professor's place after dark. I sure don't want to wind up as a bad smell in a crawl space.

What's worse, he's not the only one. He has two brothers just as spooky as he is, and get this: They're all named James! Now, there's a clue. Can you imagine what *that* household was like growing up? What do you bet his mom is sitting in a chair in the basement with spiders crawling around in her skull? Remind me to lock all the doors the next time I take a shower.

He and his brothers, they stick together, too. Say something bad about the professor, and they might sue you or something. Yeah, he's up to no good—but you could never prove it. He may be weird, but he's smart . . . some kind of a genius, or a philosopher, or an abstract thinker.

OK, OK. Maybe you're right. Maybe I'm getting carried away. He probably is some harmless old guy who just looks a little batty. He probably wouldn't hurt a fly.

But that other guy over there—the one with the two-way hat and that dumb magnifying glass? I'm even less sure about him. Some kind of stalker, I'd say. Always following the professor around. Maybe we ought to stop by the station on the way home and tell that rat-faced police inspector about him.

Well, if you're ready, let's get going.

A Chill on the Moor

Sex and Sadism in The Hound of the Baskervilles

The Hound of the Baskervilles: The most famous of all Sherlockian stories, the one that first comes to mind when the average non-Sherlockian is asked about Holmes, the most adapted of the stories in film, and the short novel that most often introduces the young reader to the world of Sherlock Holmes. It is a great adventure, an intriguing mystery, one of the great novels in literature—and, as Christopher Redmond pointed out in his excellent study, *In Bed with Sherlock Holmes*, a tale of twisted sex.

The Atavism Theme

One underlying theme of the novel is, of course, apparent to all who read it on an adult level. It is an exploration of the theory of atavism, also called reversion or intermittent heredity. In biology, atavism is the tendency to revert to ancestral type, an evolutionary throwback, with certain traits reappearing which had disappeared generations ago.

Now Conan Doyle and Dr. Watson didn't know that atavisms actually occur because genes for previously existing features—like the vestigial tail that sometimes appears in human babies—are often preserved in the DNA. For Watson and Conan Doyle, living as they did during the interval between the acceptance of evolution and the rise of our modern understanding of genetics, atavism was a term used to account for the reappearance in an individual of a trait after several generations of absence. Such an individual was sometimes called a "throwback."

But *The Hound of the Baskervilles* is not concerned a great deal with biological atavism—although Holmes' observation about Sir Hugo's family portrait and its resemblance to Stapleton certainly is an essential element to solving the mystery. This book is more concerned with the concept of atavism as an explanation of the causes of criminal behavior in an individual.

The underlying idea was popularized by the Italian criminologist Césare Lombroso in the 1870s, and Conan Doyle probably knew all about the idea. Lombroso attempted to identify physical characteristics common to criminals and labeled those he found as atavistic, "throwback" traits that determined "primitive" criminal behavior. He basically thought someone was "born criminal," an idea that most enlightened people reject today. After all, *Natural Born Killers* is a movie, not a social reality.

Lombroso's statistical evidence and the notion that physical traits determine inevitable criminality (an idea closely related to the concepts of eugenics) have long since been debunked. Even so, social scientists have refined the idea and now they sometimes talk about "resurgent atavism," a belief that people can revert to ways of thinking and acting that are throwbacks to a former time. This is especially used by sociologists in reference to violence. This theme can be found in such books as *Lord of the Flies* or such movies as *Sands of the Kalahari*.

Dr. Mortimer's list of credentials as described in Chapter 1 clearly shows us that he was a student of atavistic theory. Three of his studies are listed: "Is Disease a Reversion?" dealing with biological atavism; "Some Freaks of Atavism," dealing apparently with throwbacks; and "Do We Progress?" which seems to take on the issues of resurgent atavism.

The Bloodline Theory

This is not the only place in the canon where a similar idea pops up. Holmes held to what I would call his "Bloodline Theory." In THE GREEK INTERPRETER, Holmes and Watson had a discussion about atavism and hereditary aptitudes. He believed that his own intellectual abilities and those of his brother Mycroft were due to ancestral traits.

Holmes stated his "Bloodline Theory" this way in THE EMPTY HOUSE as he theorized about how Colonel Moran went wrong:

> There are some trees, Watson, which grow to a certain height, and then suddenly develop some unsightly eccentricity. You will see it often in humans. I have a theory that the individual represents in his development the whole procession of his ancestors, and that such a sudden turn to good or evil stands for some strong influence which came into the line of his pedigree. The person becomes, as it were, the epitome of the history of his own family.

Holmes also believed that professor Moriarty had hereditary tendencies of the most diabolical kind, that a criminal strain was to be found in his blood—or, as we know it today, in his DNA—and that this criminal strain was increased and made far, far more dangerous because of Moriarty's extraordinary mental powers. In THE LION'S MANE, Holmes said that there was "some strange, outlandish blood" in Ian Murdoch. And in THE SPECKLED BAND, the men of the Roylott family inherited violence and uncontrollable tempers.

So *The Hound of the Baskervilles* is a full blown study of atavism, of being a throwback, particularly in this case of Stapleton as a throwback to Sir Hugo Baskerville.

To make this theory work for *The Hound of the Baskervilles*, Conan Doyle didn't look to duality in an individual, as Stevenson did in *Dr. Jekyll and Mr. Hyde*. Instead, he made contrasts between members of the same family, and not only that, but between members of the same family in the same generation. This was nothing new, either—the idea goes all they way back to the Bible, to the story of Cain and Abel.

But consider the contrasts between Sir Charles and his brother Rodger Baskerville, described as "the black sheep of the family;" or between Sir Henry and his first cousin Stapleton; or even between the reliable Mrs. Barrymore and her brother, Selden the convict. Remember the description of Selden: "There could be no doubt about the beetling forehead, the sunken animal eyes . . . the face of Selden the criminal." But Mrs. Barrymore was described as "solidly respectable . . . an honest Christian woman."

Hugo Baskerville

We are familiar because of religion with the idea that both evil and good reside in us as individuals, but the idea of *The Hound* is that both evil and good run in families, and the family that demonstrates it here is the Baskerville family.

So finally, we get to that most compelling, fundamental and inescapable of all themes: Sex. Twisted, abnormal, deviant, disgusting, steaming, sweaty and yet fascinating sex. This is the real curse of the Baskervilles, the root of that sexual appetite which was to be found in Sir Hugo Baskerville, a man whose portrait, Watson would observe, "had a lurking devil in his eyes."

Consider, if you would, the very words of the Baskerville legend:

> *This Manor of Baskerville was held by Hugo of that name, nor can it be gainsaid that he was a most wild, profane, and godless man.*
>
> *This, in truth, his neighbors might have pardoned, seeing that saints have never flourished in those parts, but there was in him a certain wanton and cruel humor which made his name a byword through the West.*

> *It chanced that this Hugo came to love (if, indeed, so dark a passion may be known under so bright a name) the daughter of a yeoman who held lands near the Baskerville estate. But the young maiden, being discreet and of good repute, would ever avoid him, for she feared his evil name.*
>
> *So it came to pass that one Michaelmas this Hugo, with five or six of his idle and wicked companions, stole down upon the farm and carried off the maiden, her father and brothers being from home, as he well knew.*
>
> *When they had brought her to the Hall the maiden was placed in an upper chamber, while Hugo and his friends sat down to a long carouse, as was their nightly custom.*
>
> *Now, the poor lass upstairs was like to have her wits turned at the singing and shouting and terrible oaths which came up to her from below, for they say that the words used by Hugo Baskerville, when he was in wine, were such as might blast the man who said them.*
>
> *At last in the stress of her fear she did that which might have daunted the bravest or most active man, for by the aid of the growth of ivy which covered (and still covers) the south wall she came down from under the eaves, and so homeward across the moor, there being three leagues betwixt the Hall and her father's farm.*
>
> *It chanced that some little time later Hugo left his guests to carry food and drink—with other worse things, perchance—to his captive, and so found the cage empty and the bird escaped.*

This episode has roots in the realities of the Medieval age. The idea of the lord of the manor taking a peasant girl for his own uses is an old one; in fact, there was a time when this was considered the God-given right of the local baron. But Hugo was worse than a feudal lord who forced himself upon the peasant girls, as bad as that was. No, he was "wanton" and "cruel." The peasant girl "feared his evil name." She was made a captive, and she was terrified by the "terrible oaths" that she could hear being made downstairs by Hugo and his drunken companions.

The text hints that more than rape was intended for this girl. "Other worse things" were in store for her, we are told. With all of these clues, so starkly stated even for a more discreet time, we can probably imagine what they were, what she may have heard being promised for her in those "terrible oaths"—bondage in her captivity; sexual torture to satisfy the sadistic appetites of Sir Hugo; gang rape involving his evil companions; probably, in the end, her murder.

The poor girl did indeed escape a fate worse than death, and the spectral hound—symbolizing sexual perversion—destroyed him. Because of the possibility every Baskerville risked of a throwback to what the legend itself described as "foul passions," the author of that legend expressed this hope: "that no ban is so heavy but that by prayer and repentance it may be removed."

Rodger Baskerville

Fast forwarding for a few generations through what Watson told us was a "long line of high-blooded, fiery and masterful men," we eventually get to Sir Charles Baskerville and his brother Rodger. Sir Charles was apparently a solid citizen, a benefactor, an educated and generous man. Mortimer said that "the prosperity of the whole poor, bleak countryside depends upon his presence."

But what of his brother Rodger? We are actually told very little. Rodger Baskerville was "the black sheep of the family. He came of the old masterful Baskerville strain, and was the very image, they tell me, of the family picture of old Hugo. He made England too hot to hold him . . ."

Despite the sparseness of the information provided, these short lines reveal what this Rodger Baskerville was all about. He was, of course, a throwback to his wicked ancestor, the proof of atavistic theory in the Baskerville family. As a "black sheep," he had no regard for the rules of society and probably very little in the way of conscience. As the image of old Hugo, he apparently possessed those "foul passions" which had cursed the Baskerville family—that is, deviant sexual appetites. And we can imagine how those foul passions made England "too hot to hold him"—sexual sadism run amok, perhaps a particularly violent episode involving a servant girl or even a prostitute.

Something like this could be hushed up for an aristocratic family like the Baskervilles—for a price. However, in addition to a significant amount of money in the right hands, that price would include getting the "black sheep" out of England, never to return.

As for his supposed death of yellow fever, we must, I suppose, take the account at face value. But Roger didn't leave his character behind him, and his death from venereal disease or a hot-blooded Latin version of family justice after another episode of sexual excess seems much more likely.

Queer Place, The Moor

All of this leads us, inevitably, to Stapleton, the son of this Rodger Baskerville, and like his father the throwback to old Sir Hugo. He was, in modern lingo, really "messed up," and the story of *The Hound of the Baskervilles* paints an extremely troubling picture of him.

In doing so, the novel has two very important allegories that we should bear in mind throughout. The hound itself, as already mentioned, represents the sexual perversions that were also the personal demons of the Baskerville family—their real curse. The moor and especially the Grimpen Mire are more broadly symbolic. They represent the uncharted and unmentionable urges that provide a habitat where the hound, representing those actual sexual aberrations, can exist. This makes Stapleton's comment much more ominous when he says to Dr. Watson:

> Ever since I have been here I have been conscious of shadows all round me. Life has become like the great Grimpen Mire, with little green patches everywhere into which one may sink and with no guide to point the track.

Another passage from chapter 7 seems even more chilling:

> It is a wonderful place, the moor . . . You never tire of the moor. You cannot think of the wonderful secret which it contains. It is so vast, and so barren, and so mysterious . . . But my taste led me to explore every part of the country round, and I should think there are few men who know it better than I do.

As the sound of that bittern booming is heard, Stapleton looks at Watson "with a curious expression on his face. "Queer place, the moor! said he."

Stapleton the Collector

First, let us consider Stapleton, the cruel sadist. To understand him in this light, we must look at what might be considered to be an innocent pastime, or only a cover for Stapleton's false identity. He was an insect collector. Now, most insect collectors are harmless hobbyists, kind of nerdy perhaps, interested only in an academic way in a fascinating area of learning, obsessive in their collecting, apt to get excited about anything related to the world of their peculiar enthusiasm. Come to think of it, they are a lot like Sherlockians.

But the very act of collecting insects involves something more. The capture of the insect, handling it, having power over it, watching it slowly die as it is suffocated, as breath is slowly taken away from it, the final flutter of its wings, pinning it to a board as something of a trophy. The perfect hobby for a man of sadistic bent.

John Fowles, a fine author who himself wrote an introduction to *The Hound of the Baskervilles*, wrote a novel titled *The Collector* about a lonely young man, Frederick Clegg, who works as a clerk in a city hall, and collects butterflies in his spare time. Clegg is obsessed with Miranda Grey, an upper-class art student. He decides to add her to his "collection" of pretty, petrified objects, and after careful preparations, he kidnaps Miranda using chloroform and locks her up in the cellar of his house.

There are several cases in which serial killers, spree killers, kidnappers, and other criminals have claimed that *The Collector* was the basis, the inspiration, or even the justification for their crimes. A character named Leonard Lake was utterly obsessed with *The Collector*, and he and an accomplice abducted, raped, tortured and finally killed two teenage girls. Another killer, Robert Berdella held his victims captive and photographed their torture before killing them. He claimed that the film version of *The Collector* had been his inspiration when he was a teenager.

Oddly, Fowles never drew the parallel between his creation and Stapleton. What a great addition to his introduction to *The Hound* that would have been.

So Stapleton's collection was not benign at all, it was a manifestation of his sadistic bent, not too far removed from the sadistic pleasure that Jephro Rucastle's horrible little boy took in the "smack, smack, smack" of cockroaches with a slipper in THE COPPER BEECHES. But evidence of Stapleton's fiendish attitude toward animal life comes through loud an clear in the account of the moor ponies as witnessed by Dr. Watson. The allegorical meaning of the Grimpen Mire, the uncharted territory of sexual deviance, is evident and gives the passage a chilling tone:

> *Stapleton laughed. That is the great Grimpen Mire, said he. A false step yonder means death to man or beast.*
>
> *Only yesterday I saw one of the moor ponies wander into it. He never came out. I saw his head for quite a long time craning out of the bog-hole, but it sucked him down at last.*
>
> *Even in dry seasons it is a danger to cross it, but after these autumn rains it is an awful place. And yet I can find my way to the very heart of it and return alive. By George, there is another of those miserable ponies!*
>
> *Something brown was rolling and tossing among the green sedges. Then a long, agonized, writhing neck shot upward and a dreadful cry*

echoed over the moor. It turned me cold with horror, but my companion's nerves seemed to be stronger than mine.

It's gone! said he. The mire has him. Two in two days, and many more, perhaps, for they get in the way of going there in the dry weather and never know the difference until the mire has them in its clutches. It's a bad place, the great Grimpen Mire.

The lack of feeling for the ponies, and the apparent glee he has in their tortured deaths, speaks volumes about the psychological state of Stapleton. He was a cold-blooded sadist, without a doubt. And this attitude toward animals in children has long been recognized as an indicator of similar attitudes toward other people later in life—a "rehearsal," if you will, for later behavior.

Stapleton the Bisexual Pedophile

Stapleton is described by Watson as "a small, slim, clean-shaven, prim-faced man, flaxen haired and lean-jawed, between thirty and forty years of age, dressed in a gray suit and wearing a straw hat. A tin box for botanical specimens hung round his shoulder, and he carried a green butterfly net in one of his hands." Now this is certainly no masculine picture that is drawn for us. An effeminate figure, engaged in a distinctly non-masculine pastime, with something akin to a purse hanging off his shoulder. He wasn't exactly Boy George, but perhaps he resembled David Bowie just a little.

Significantly, Watson gives us a hint, a suggestion. Stapleton was, he said, "neutral-tinted, with light hair and grey eyes." But just what is Watson suggesting by the term "neutral-tinted" or by the term he used later in the story, "colorless?"

The answer may lie in an episode from Stapleton's past, a time when he and Beryl were posing as "Mr. and Mrs. Vandeleur, who at the time kept St. Oliver's School." This school is mentioned no less than four times in the narrative, but Stapleton and Holmes offered different accounts. First, Stapleton:

> I had a school . . . It was in the north country. The work to a man of my temperament was mechanical and uninteresting, but the privilege of living with youth, of helping to mould those young minds, and of impressing them with one's own character and ideals was very dear to me. However, the fates were against us. A serious epidemic broke out in the school and three of the boys

died. It never recovered from the blow, and much of my capital was irretrievably swallowed up. And yet, if it were not for the loss of the charming companionship of the boys, I could rejoice over my own misfortune.

But Holmes told the story a little differently:

> [Stapleton] was once a schoolmaster in the north of England. Now, there is no one more easy to trace than a schoolmaster... A little investigation showed me that a school had come to grief under atrocious circumstances.
>
> He changed his name to Vandeleur and fled to England, where he established a school in the east of Yorkshire. His reason for attempting this special line of business was that he had struck up an acquaintance with a consumptive tutor upon the voyage home, and that he had used this man's ability to make the undertaking a success.
>
> Fraser, the tutor, died however, and the school which had begun well sank from disrepute into infamy.
>
> The Vandeleurs found it convenient to change their name to Stapleton, and he brought the remains of his fortune, his schemes for the future, and his taste for entomology to the south of England.

A school for boys, enjoying some degree of success, came to endure "atrocious circumstances," "disrepute," and "infamy?" Why? What would cause such a problem to happen?

The obvious answer is sexual exploitation of the boys. The "atrocious circumstances" would be the reports, whispered at first, desperately covered up by victims and victimizer alike. The "disrepute" would come when this sexual abuse became common knowledge. Finally, "infamy" came with a public scandal associated with the deaths of three of the students—victims of the kind of twisted sexual abuse that we know Stapleton to be capable of committing. The school came to grief, and Stapleton changed his name and escaped from justice.

According to *The Merck Manual of Diagnosis and Therapy*, prepubescent boys are preferred by bisexual adult pedophiles. Was this the barely perceptible suggestion of Watson's description of Stapleton as "neutral-tinted" or "colorless," that his sexual preferences were apt to go in either direction?

Stapleton the Masochist

But what of Stapleton's relationship with both his wife Beryl and his mistress, Laura Lyons? Clearly, he had the ability to completely dominate them. "Both of them," said Holmes, "were under his influence, and he had nothing to fear from them."

But Stapleton had different uses for the two women. Beryl was the object of his desire to dominate, to control, to act out the sadistic tendencies he learned with his butterflies and the moor ponies and refined with the poor boys of St. Oliver's School. Laura Lyons was different. She was the object of his desire to *be* dominated, to assuage his guilt, perhaps, with pain.

Let's take Laura Lyons first. Holmes noted that there was what he called a "close intimacy" and a "complete understanding" between Laura and Stapleton. Remember, she had married an artist without her father's consent, but he deserted her; and Dr. Mortimer commented that, "The fault, from what I hear, may not have been entirely on one side." Her father had disowned her, and she was in fairly desperate circumstances.

Mortimer made an interesting comment. He said, "Whatever she may have deserved, one could not allow her to go hopelessly to the bad." Now, going bad, for a woman in the Victorian era, pretty much meant one thing: prostitution. It was common at the time, and quite a few women turned to it as a last resort for survival. In a relatively small community, that was to be prevented, and several people in that community decided to help her earn what they called "an honest living."

To this sad situation comes a predator, Stapleton. He saw, undoubtedly what Watson saw when he first met her: "The first impression left by Mrs. Lyons was one of extreme beauty . . . But the second was criticism. There was something subtly wrong with the face, some coarseness of expression, some hardness, perhaps, of eye, some looseness of lip which marred its perfect beauty . . . something relentless and defiant in her manner."

Laura Lyons was the reckless rock star Madonna of her day. One can just see her in black leather, cracking that whip, satisfying Stapleton's bizarre appetites even as he supplied her financial needs and manipulated her emotionally. "By representing himself as a single man he acquired complete influence over her," Holmes explained, "and he gave her to understand that in the event of her obtaining a divorce from her husband he would marry her." This gave him the chance to get at Sir Charles, of course. But if he satisfied a few of his blackest passions in the meantime, well, all the better for him.

Stapleton the Sadist

Stapleton's cruelty, of course, was focused especially upon his wife Beryl. That he had her intimidated and fearful of him, that he dominated her, is demonstrated throughout the book. Consider Watson's description of the two of them together:

> [Stapleton] gives the idea of hidden fires. He has certainly a very marked influence over [Beryl], for I have seen her continually glance at him as she talked as if seeking approbation for what she said . . . There is a dry glitter in his eyes and a firm set of his thin lips, which goes with a positive and possibly a harsh nature.

Later, says Watson, "Stapleton turned upon his heel and beckoned in a preemptory way to his sister, who, after an irresolute glance at Sir Henry, walked off by the side of her brother."

We learn later, from Holmes, that Beryl had frequently been beaten by Stapleton. She feared her husband, and that fear was founded on "brutal ill-treatment." But she obeyed, because Stapleton's influence over her, in Holmes's words, "may have been love, or may have been fear, or very possibly both, since they are by no means incompatible."

But the real evidence of Stapleton's truly frightening domination of Beryl, a domination that veered into the realm of sadistic sexual abuse, the climax to Stapleton's twisted life and forbidden appetites, came when Holmes, Watson and Lestrade burst into the upper floor bedroom—where else?—of Merrepit House. It is perhaps the most sexually charged passage in all of the Sherlockian canon:

> *A faint moaning and rustling came from within. Holmes struck the door just over the lock with the flat of his foot and it flew open. Pistol in hand, we all three rushed into the room.*
>
> *But there was no sign within it of that desperate and defiant villain whom we expected to see. Instead we were faced by an object so strange and so unexpected that we stood for a moment staring at it in amazement.*
>
> *The room had been fashioned into a small museum, and the walls were lined by a number of glass-topped cases full of that collection of butterflies and moths the formation of which had been the relaxation of this complex and dangerous man.*
>
> *In the centre of this room there was an upright beam, which had been placed at some period as a support for the old worm-eaten baulk of timber which spanned the roof.*

> *To this post a figure was tied, so swathed and muffled in the sheets which had been used to secure it that one could not for the moment tell whether it was that of a man or a woman. One towel passed round the throat and was secured at the back of the pillar. Another covered the lower part of the face, and over it two dark eyes—eyes full of grief and shame and a dreadful questioning—stared back at us. In a minute we had torn off the gag, unswathed the bonds, and Mrs. Stapleton sank upon the floor in front of us.*
>
> *As her beautiful head fell upon her chest I saw the clear red weal of a whiplash across her neck.*
>
> *The brute! cried Holmes. Here, Lestrade, your brandy-bottle! Put her in the chair! She has fainted from ill-usage and exhaustion . . .*
>
> *Oh, this villain! See how he has treated me! She shot her arms out from her sleeves, and we saw with horror that they were all mottled with bruises.*
>
> *But this is nothing—nothing! It is my mind and soul that he has tortured and defiled. I could endure it all, ill-usage, solitude, a life of deception, everything, as long as I could still cling to the hope that I had his love, but now I know that in this also I have been his dupe and his tool.*

This dramatic scene has been notoriously depicted on the Bantam paperback edition of *The Hound of the Baskervilles,* and it has everything: imprisonment, bondage, phallic symbolism, beatings, whipping, branding, shame, emotional subjugation. It takes place in the bedroom. She was unidentifiable as either man or woman. All of Stapleton's sexual disorders converged in this, the last of his outrages.

Unmasking the Villain

The ancestral portraits, of course, gave Holmes the clue he needed. Stapleton, alias Roger Baskerville, was indeed the throwback to his evil, black-hearted ancestor, Sir Hugo. The theory of social atavism was proved, at least in the minds of Holmes and Watson, by this particular villain. And Stapleton, if anything, was the most depraved of all the Baskervilles. If Holmes' "Bloodline Theory" held true, Stapleton was the end result of all the bad traits of all the Baskervilles who went before him. And from what we have learned, he must have been the worst: a sado-masochistic bisexual pedophile and psychotic murderer. One cannot get much more out of the bounds of normal behavior than that.

That Stapleton was also a burglar and common killer almost seem to be among his lesser evils. He was a dangerous man, indeed, as Watson described him, "a creature of infinite patience and craft, with a smiling face and a murderous heart."

Conclusion

"Do We Progress?" asks Dr. Mortimer in one of those publications that set the tone, and the theme, for *The Hound of the Baskervilles*. We know that Stapleton did not progress. His destructive sexual appetites led to his downfall. "Somewhere in the heart of the Grimpen Mire, down in the foul slime of the huge morass which had sucked him in, this cold and cruel-hearted man is forever buried." We cannot forget what the Grimpen Mire represents.

But what about the rest of us? Do we progress? Holmes and Watson themselves had to be wary of the Grimpen Mire and of what it represented. As Watson observed, "The longer one stays here, the more does the spirit of the moor sink into one's soul."

Furthermore, as the two friends hunted Stapleton, they themselves were being hunted: "Its tenacious grip plucked at our heels as we walked, and when we sank into it, it was if some malignant hand was tugging us down into those obscene depths, so grim and purposeful was the clutch in which it held us."

Maybe, for us all, avoiding our own version of the Grimpen Mire will be a worthy and life-long quest.

Horror of the Hound

I

Holmes receives a visitor, and
Hears a gruesome thing:
Heart has failed a high-born squire.
Heir is next, it seems.

Hideous was the look of terror
Hardened on Sir Charles' face.
How could such a thing befall him; what
Happened in that lonely place?

(Hugo was an evil lord:
Hunted down a lass, and
Hexed a noble family, now
Haunted by the past.)

Hardly had Sir Charles succumbed,
Hands outstretched, they found, a
Harbinger of doom: the footprints—
Hints of a gigantic hound.

> *Hell has loosed its denizen,*
> *Hound of massive size,*
> *Howling for the Baskervilles, the*
> *Horror of their lives.*

II

Hale and hearty was young Henry,
Handsome. Strong and more.
Half or less he credits legends,
Honors not the ancient lore.

Hotel porter's lost a boot.
Hansom gives a chase.
Hat and beard disguise the man, but
Hatred's on his face.

Honest Watson takes a trip.
Henry is his charge. The
Hall of Baskervilles at last; the
House is grim and large.

Hiking 'cross the treacherous moor—
Heath-covered is the land—they
Hear a sound that only makes the
Hair and hackles stand.

> *Hell has loosed its denizen,*
> *Hound of massive size,*
> *Howling for the Baskervilles, the*
> *Horror of their lives.*

III

Hour past midnight. Attic room.
Housekeeper and her mate
Hail her brother, Princeton's claim,
Hiding from his fate.

High above the Dartmoor gloom, a
Hilltop figure stands;
Human agent on the prowl,
Hushed form in barren lands.

Halloa! Calls Watson on the moor,
Hunting for a clue. A
Hut contains good Sherlock Holmes, who'll
Help him muddle through.

Hue and moan alert this pair; they
Hasten toward the cry. But
Hope cannot the convict reach,
Hurled from the cliff to die.

> *Hell has loosed its denizen,*
> *Hound of massive size,*
> *Howling for the Baskervilles, the*
> *Horror of their lives.*

IV

Healthy romance makes Sir Henry
Hearken to dear Beryl's charms;
Humbly plans his visit to her
Heedless of his friends' alarms.

Having finished with his call,
Homeward bound Sir Henry treads.
Hapless victim, still unknowing,
Hence his deep and nameless dread.

Hanging dense and low, the fog
Hampers those who guard the trail.
Hungry now, the blood-mad brute
Hurries on with nightmare wail.

Horrible, the hound descends, but
Holmes and Watson make their aim.
Halted in the act of death, the
Handiwork of evil's slain.

> *Hell has lost its denizen,*
> *Hound of massive size,*
> *Howling for the Baskervilles, the*
> *Horror of their lives.*

V

Heaving breaths of great relief, the
Heroes search for Stapleton.
Husband he, not Beryl's brother,
Hard and cruel conspiring one.

History had been his partner.
Hubris had his passion fed.
Heritage he shared with Henry.
Hung his plot on kinship's thread.

Hobbled not by conscience calling,
Harshly had he trained the hound.
Handled it with vicious motive,
Harbored it beneath the ground.

Haggard failure, villain flees,
Harassed by those who truth desire.
Heavy is his step; he'll spend
Hereafter 'neath the Grimpen Mire.

> *Hell has claimed its denizens,*
> *Hound and man despised,*
> *Howling for the Baskervilles, the*
> *Horror of their lives.*

The Rule of Three

The Significance of Sherlockian Trios

Three is a magic number.

Now, you may not believe in magic, and you may not be superstitious, and you may roll your eyes at such ideas. You probably got a little bit disgusted in your college English or psychology classes when your professor insisted on finding "hidden meanings" in little everyday actions, or nursery rhymes, or classic novels, or even adventure stories about a certain consulting detective in Victorian London.

Sherlockians, especially, don't believe in magic numbers, do we? But there is no denying that down through the centuries—in theology, in science, in mathematics, in literature and indeed in just about every aspect of human existence—the number three has a special place. And the Sherlock Holmes stories are no exception. In almost every one of the tales, trios of individuals, time periods measured by threes, or three-fold objects play a significant role.

The Victorian Vogue

In Victorian times, magic numbers, especially the number three and numbers divisible by it, fascinated the Victorians. Three was in vogue, then. In fact, there was an intellectual fad involving the number three at the height of the Victorian era. Thomas and Jean Sebeok go so far as to say that "some of the more brilliant Victorians" were "tormented" by the number. The well-educated—the thinkers—tried to find some kind of trio in just about every aspect of learning. It was all the rage, and this was the very time when Conan Doyle was writing his best Sherlock Holmes stories.

Of course, there are all sorts of significant threes in science and religion. For instance, the American logician Charles Sanders Peirce tried to distill his understanding of the world into a trinity of *It* (the material world), *Thou* (the world of the mind), and *I* (the abstract, or spiritual world), but he even speculated that people would think that he attached "a superstitious or fanciful importance to the number three."

Sigmund Freud divided the human mind into *Ego, Id,* and *Superego*. And in Christian theology, God is a Trinity of *Father, Son* and *Holy Spirit*. The book of Genesis tells us that human beings are made "in the image of God" with a similar tripartite existence of *body* (our physical selves), *spirit* (that is, life or animation) and *soul* (our immortal aspect, which sets us apart from the animals).

Well, all of that is fodder for philosophers. It is interesting for those who like to ponder such things. But we are more concerned with a more down to earth examination of Arthur Conan Doyle, or Dr. John H. Watson, and the significance that "three" has in the Sherlockian saga.

The Influence of Literary Threes

As a true man of letters, Conan Doyle would not have been immune from the Victorian era's intellectual "craze" for the number three. And a case can be made that some famous threes of literature had an impact on his writings.

C. Auguste Dupin. Conan Doyle was tremendously influenced by Edgar Allen Poe and his detective, C. Auguste Dupin, and he acknowledged that debt numerous times. Yes, he allowed Sherlock Holmes to dismiss Dupin as "a very inferior fellow" in *A Study in Scarlet,* but Conan Doyle himself asked aloud at a testimonial dinner in 1911, "Where was the detective story until Poe breathed the breath of life into it?" And how many times did Dupin appear? In exactly three stories: THE MURDERS IN THE RUE MORGUE, THE MYSTERY OF MARIE ROGÊT, and THE PURLOINED LETTER.

Holmes, of course, appeared in far more stories than Dupin—60 to be exact; that is, three score. Of those three score stories, exactly three feature the number three in the title: THE THREE GARRIDEBS, THE THREE STUDENTS and THE THREE GABLES. (I do not count THE MISSING THREE-QUARTER, as this term means something else entirely.) So, while other numbers appear in Sherlockian titles only once, three—the magic number three—significantly appears three different times.

Three Blind Mice. Literature through the ages features countless threesomes. Even nursery rhymes frequently include trios of one kind or another. Besides providing the theme song for the Three Stooges, THREE BLIND MICE is a very old Mother Goose rhyme. Arthur Conan Doyle's father even drew illustrations for it. There are no blind mice in the Sherlockian stories, but there *are* three blind beetles—or, at least, people who are described as blind beetles: Jim Browner of THE CARDBOARD BOX,

Hall Pycroft of THE STOCKBROKER'S CLERK and Sherlock Holmes himself in THE PRIORY SCHOOL.

The Three Little Pigs. Another old English nursery rhyme is THE THREE LITTLE PIGS, in which the Big Bad Wolf on three different occasions participates in this classic exchange:

> *"Little pig, little pig, let me come in."*
> *"No, no, by the hair on my chinny chin chin."*

These pigs were fat, you see, and they had three chins each. Thus, the "chinny chin chin" rather than just chin. And it just so happens that Holmes and Watson encountered exactly three characters in the course of their adventures with multiple chins. The "three little pigs" of the Sherlockian canon were:

- Jephro Rucastle of THE COPPER BEECHES, who had "a great heavy chin which rolled down in fold upon fold over his throat."
- Culverton Smith of THE DYING DETECTIVE, who possessed "a great yellow face, coarse-grained and greasy, with heavy, double-chin."
- Dr. Thorneycroft Huxtable of THE PRIORY SCHOOL, whose "rolling chins" (as Watson observed) were unshaven.

The Three Musketeers. One of the most significant and important of the literary influences on the Sherlockian canon comes from a classic French adventure novel, *The Three Musketeers* by Alexandre Dumas. This passage comes from Chapter 26, THE WIFE OF ATHOS, in which Athos tells the following sad tale to d'Artagnan:

> *One of my friends* [he was speaking about himself], *a count of the province of Berry . . . at twenty-five years of age fell in love with a girl of sixteen. She was as beautiful as fancy can paint . . . She did not please, she intoxicated.*
>
> *She lived in a small town with her brother, a curate—both had recently come into the country. Nobody knew whence they came, and on seeing her so lovely, and her brother so pious, no one thought of making inquiry. They were said, however, to be of good extraction. My friend, who was seigneur of the country, might have taken the girl by force if he had wished—for he was the master. Unfortunately, he was an honest man; he married her . . .*
>
> *Well, one day when she was hunting with her husband . . . she fell from her horse and fainted. The count flew to her help, and as she*

> *appeared to be oppressed by her clothes, he ripped them open with his poniard and in so doing laid bare her shoulder. D'Artagnan . . . guess what she had on her shoulder? . . .*
>
> *A fleur-de-lis . . . She was branded!*
>
> *[The count] was of the highest nobility. He had on his estates the right of high and low tribunals. He tore the dress of the countess to pieces. He tied her hands behind her and hanged her to a tree . . . That has cured me of beautiful and loving women . . .*
>
> *I inquired after [the brother] for the purposes of hanging him, too. But he was beforehand with me. He had quitted the curacy the night previous . . . He was doubtless the first lover and the accomplice of the fair lady. A worthy man who had pretended to be a curate for the purpose of getting his mistress married and securing her a position. He has been hanged and quartered, I hope.*

The parallels of this story from *The Three Musketeers* and the account of the Stapletons and Sir Henry from *The Hound of the Baskervilles* are too obvious to ignore.

Both stories feature an unmarried young nobleman, the master of his large estates—Athos (in reality, the Comte de la Fère) in *The Three Musketeers* and Sir Henry Baskerville in *The Hound*. Both of these noblemen are the victim of a scam: a husband (or lover) and wife team masquerading as a respectable brother and sister—although no one really knows about the background of either couple. Both Athos and Sir Henry are infatuated with, and propose to marry, the supposed sister—the evil Milady in *The Three Musketeers* and the harder-to-define Beryl in *The Hound*.

The day of discovery has parallel features as well. Milady was tied and hanged to a tree. Beryl was discovered at Merripit House tied to "an upright beam" with "one towel passed round the throat and . . . secured at the back of the pillar."

Milady had been branded as a criminal with a fleur-de-lis. Beryl Stapleton "sank upon the floor" when she was found, and Watson "saw the clear red weal of a whiplash across her neck."

In both cases, the brother figure fled for his life. The fate of both theoretically was a fitting death; but in reality, no one knows as an absolute certainty what happened to either one of them.

Thus, *The Three Musketeers,* one of the most famous of classics, a book that Conan Doyle no doubt read many times, contributed many of the essential elements of *The Hound of the Baskervilles*. And the number three played a significant role in the development of the canon.

Three for Sherlock

For Sherlock Holmes himself, the number three recurred frequently over the years, and there can be little doubt that it was a significant number to him.

We think of Holmes as part of a "dynamic duo," with he and Watson operating much like Batman and Robin. But just as Batman and Robin found Alfred the butler essential, so did Watson and Holmes depend upon the third resident of 221B Baker Street, Mrs. Hudson. On many occasions, Holmes and Watson joined with some other person in temporary alliances—for instance, the trio of Holmes, Watson and Lestrade lay in wait for the Hound of the Baskervilles.

Also, Holmes tells us in THE DISAPPEARANCE OF LADY FRANCES CARFAX that he employed "a small, but very efficient organization" to assist him in his detective practice. There are only three adult members of this "agency"—as Holmes called it—who are named: Mercer, who appears in THE CREEPING MAN; Shinwell Johnson, who appears in THE ILLUSTRIOUS CLIENT; and "Langdale Pike," who appears in THE THREE GABLES.

Holmes identified "three qualities necessary for the ideal detective"—observation, deduction and knowledge (*The Sign of Four*). There were three women named Violet whose lives intersected with his own. He indulged in cocaine "three times a day for many months" (also in *The Sign of Four*); the dressing-gowns he wore came in three different colors; and he considered a particularly difficult puzzle to be "quite a three-pipe problem" (THE RED-HEADED LEAGUE). Yes, the number three had a way of revisiting Sherlock Holmes throughout his career.

Gangs of Three

"There are other gangs of three," declared Inspector Stanley Hopkins, speaking of villains in THE ABBEY GRANGE. And so there were. By and large, throughout the canon, the number three was not positive. This also has literary precedent. For instance, in Shakespeare, three witches opened the tale of Macbeth, and they had a great little chant:

> *Double, double, toil and trouble;*
> *Fire, burn; and caldron, bubble.*

The three ghosts of *A Christmas Carol* by Charles Dickens foretold the coming doom of Scrooge—providing he did not mend his ways. Likewise, in the Sherlockian saga, a group of three most often represented danger, doom, or disaster.

The story that demonstrates this best is probably THE FIVE ORANGE PIPS, which, despite its title, is full to the brim with ominous uses of three.

The Openshaws were threatened by messages bearing three letters: KKK. The Ku Klux Klan claimed three victims in England: Col. John Openshaw, the traitor to the Klan; his brother Joseph Openshaw; and John Openshaw, Joseph's son and Holmes' client. These three murders were preceded by three letters of warning, one from Pondicherry, one from Dundee, and one from London. The second victim, Joseph Openshaw, died on the third day after receiving the warning of the five orange pips. The murders were committed by a gang of three: Captain James Calhoun and his two mates, all of whom apparently perished in the sinking of the *Lone Star*.

So there are these deadly groups of three in this story: 1) the three letters in KKK; 2) the three murdered men; 3) the three letters of warning; 4) three days between Joseph's letter and his murder; and 5) the three culprits. Five threes. THE FIVE ORANGE PIPS.

Yet another "gang of three" committed a murder for revenge in THE RESIDENT PATIENT, when Blessington was hanged by his former accomplices, the remnants of the Worthington Bank Gang—three men, to be exact, named Biddle, Hayward and Moffat. Just as Calhoun and his Klansmen conveniently died at sea, so did these three murderers. They supposedly perished in "the ill-fated *Norah Creina*, which was lost some years ago with all hands on the Portuguese coast."

Other gangs of three include:

- the three Sikhs, who gave Jonathan Small a really not-too-difficult choice of either joining them or getting his throat cut in *The Sign of Four*.
- the three robbers (of an original six, that is, 3 + 3) from the Ballarat Gang, who robbed the gold convoy traveling to Melbourne, Australia. Three of the gang were killed in that robbery, but John Turner—once known as "Black Jack of Ballarat"—was one of the three survivors, as described in THE BOSCOMBE VALLEY MYSTERY.
- the three conspirators of THE SOLITARY CYCLIST—namely Bob Carruthers, Jack Woodley and the defrocked clergyman Williamson—who tried to force Miss Violet Smith into marriage.

- the "three Randalls, consisting of a father and his two sons, known as "the Lewisham gang of burglars." They were real crooks, and their existence in the area of the Abbey Grange provided cover for the real killer of the abusive Sir Eustace Brackenstall. (That was a case in which Holmes let the culprit, Captain Croker, go free—he subscribed to a legal defense deemed permissible in my part of the country: "He needed killin'.")
- the three Central Americans—the exiled dictator Don Juan Murillo (known as the Tiger of San Pedro), his secretary Lopez, and his man-servant José—who worked together to entrap and murder Aloysius Garcia, the son of one of his bitterest political enemies in WISTERIA LODGE.

And "gangs of three" did not always have to be people. After all, John Ferrier and little Lucy were stalked by "three solemn buzzards" in *A Study in Scarlet*.

The Rule of Three

In *The Sign of Four*, to illustrate a point to Dr. Watson, Sherlock Holmes mentioned "a sum in the rule of three." Now, the "Rule of Three" is a part of the science of mathematics, and it is a pretty arcane concept to most of us. But the gist of it is this: a logical progression of factors leads to a certain result. Holmes compared his own method of reasoning to the mathematical "Rule of Three."

My theory is that there is a "Rule of Three" for the Sherlockian stories. It has nothing to do with mathematics really, and it is not the same "Rule of Three" that mathematicians use. But it does have a formula, and the formula is:

$$absence + 3 = death$$

Before specific examples are examined, a review of the basic elements of the Sherlockian "Rule of Three" formula might be helpful. "Absence" is pretty much self explanatory; it refers to the absence of some person from another person or place. The "three" refers always to some period of time—three hours, three days, three weeks, or three years. And the death can occur at the beginning of the period of absence, or at the end, or perhaps even both.

So the thesis is this: In the Sherlockian stories, any absence, measured in time periods of three, is connected with death in some manner. This is a peculiarity of the Sherlockian canon, but it seems to hold true whenever the pertinent elements appear.

A Study in Scarlet. The Sherlockian "Rule of Three" appears with force in the very first story, *A Study in Scarlet*. Things were looking grim for John Ferrier and little Lucy when those three buzzards just mentioned were circling around them. Lucy's mother had been absent—because of death—for three days, during which time Ferrier had done all he knew how, forging on without rest, and resigning himself at last to the likelihood that they would die. The arrival of the Mormons saved their lives, but the formula was already in effect.

The absence: Lucy's mother. *The time*: three days. *The death*: Lucy's mother, in reality, at the beginning; and their own, in expectation, at the end.

THE BOSCOMBE VALLEY MYSTERY. James McCarthy "had been away from home for three days at Bristol, and had only just returned." We know, of course, that he was with his barmaid wife, and "his father did not know where he was." When James returned, his father—Charles McCarthy—was murdered.

The absence: James McCarthy. *The time*: three days. *The death*: Charles McCarthy.

THE MUSGRAVE RITUAL. Richard Brunton, the butler in the Musgrave household, disappeared completely and unexpectedly, leaving all of his property behind him. His former fiancée, Rachel Howells, lay "ill, sometimes delirious, sometimes hysterical," for three nights, then she herself disappeared. We learn later that she had trapped Brunton in the treasure crypt and left him to die, The formula again holds true.

The absence: Brunton the butler, and also Rachel Howells. *The time*: three nights. *The death*: again, Brunton.

THE GREEK INTERPRETER. The evil conspirators, Harold Latimer and Wilson Kemp, imprisoned Paul Kratides in an attempt to gain control of his fortune. Because of the clever questioning of the Greek interpreter, Mr. Melas, we know that Kratides was held for three weeks, but he was murdered after his torture and starvation.

The absence: Paul Kratides, who was kidnapped. *The time*: three weeks. *The death*: again, Kratides.

THE PRIORY SCHOOL is overflowing with periods of three. Dr. Thorneycroft Huxtable lurched into Sherlock Holmes' rooms three days after the disappearance of the young Arthur, Lord Saltire, the son of the Duke of Holdernesse. Heidegger, the German master, had disappeared at the very same time. Huxtable told Holmes that the boy had come to the Priory School only "three weeks ago." The investigation by Sherlock

Holmes lost little time in turning up the body of Herr Heidegger. After that discovery, James Wilder begged the Duke for "three days longer" to keep his secret; Reuben Hayes was given the opportunity to flee; and the Duke agreed to leave young Arthur in the charge of Mrs. Hayes for another three days (although that time period was never fulfilled).

As for the Sherlockian "Rule of Three," there are numerous applications. The death, of course, was that of the German master, Heidegger. But there are five different absences, all associated with time periods of three, and all with a beginning or ending point at Heidegger's death.

THE VALLEY OF FEAR. In the epilogue of *The Valley of Fear,* Holmes received the news that Birdy Edwards, who was still posing as Jack Douglas and who had started for South Africa aboard the *Palmyra* three weeks earlier, apparently had been lost overboard during a storm. Holmes claimed that he was murdered by the agents of Moriarty. (I, personally, have never believed that—Edwards was too wily, too experienced and had survived too much to be caught so flat-footed. This supposed disappearance was more likely a ruse on Birdy Edwards' part to put the whole business behind him once and for all.)

But, be that as it may, the Sherlockian "Rule of Three" holds true. *The absence*: Birdy Edwards and his wife Ivy from England. *The time*: three weeks *The death*: Birdy Edwards.

The Death and Resurrection of Sherlock Holmes

For all of these examples of gangs of three, uses of three and the Sherlockian "Rule of Three"—and many others, no doubt, could be cited—none is so profound nor so important as the application to Sherlock Holmes himself in the story of his dramatic battle with Professor Moriarty, his supposed death, and his astonishing return to London. THE FINAL PROBLEM and THE EMPTY HOUSE are so replete with references to three that the whole subject could be reduced to the study of this narrative as told in these two stories.

To begin with, take Moriarty himself. There was not just one Moriarty. There were three—three brothers Moriarty! Two of whom, and probably all three, were apparently named James. Now, this is almost supernatural. A trinity of evil facing the forces of good, as personified in Sherlock Holmes. Even today, we look at evil in threesomes, even in geopolitical terms—the Axis Powers of World War II (Germany, Italy and Japan) and President Bush's more recently-defined "Axis of Evil" (Iraq, Iran and North Korea).

Now, the Sherlockian "Rule of Three" as it applies here probably leaped into the mind of every person considering this thesis as soon as I defined it. Holmes supposedly died at the Reichenbach Falls and was presumed dead for three years before he appeared before the astonished, but overjoyed, Dr. Watson. The comparison with the most obvious example of death and resurrection in a period of three—that of Christ, who lay three days in the tomb—has been made by others. I have never really been comfortable with it. But as far as the story of Sherlock Holmes is concerned, the "Rule of Three" again is confirmed.

The absence: Sherlock Holmes, traveling the world, supposedly dead. *The time*: three years. *The death*: Moriarty, to begin that period; and Ronald Adair, to end it. This is the ultimate, the most important, the archetypical application of the Sherlockian "Rule of Three" in the entire canon.

But that is not the only example of the "Rule of Three" in the story of the duel at the Reichenbach Falls. Remember Watson's own original account of being lured away from the scene of the battle between Holmes and Moriarty, as recorded in THE FINAL PROBLEM. "It had taken me an hour to come down," he said. "For all my efforts two more had passed before I found myself at the falls of Reichenbach once more."

The absence: Watson's, from the Reichenbach Falls. *The time*: a total of three hours. *The death*: that of Moriarty and, as far as Watson knew, of Holmes.

To punctuate the use of this essential application of the "Rule of Three," the entire two-story narrative is chock full of other uses of the number three.

- Watson opens his record by noting that "in the year 1890, there were only three cases of which I retain any record"
- Holmes declared that, at the end of three months of his most intense efforts, "I was forced to confess that I had at last met an antagonist who was my intellectual equal."
- But finally, Holmes says, "the last steps were taken, and three days only were wanted to complete the business."
- Three attempts were made on Holmes' life after his confrontation with Moriarty at Baker street: 1) he was nearly run down by a two-horse van; 2) a brick was flung at him from a rooftop; and 3) he was attacked by "a rough with a bludgeon."
- Watson was instructed to take the third hansom cab when he departed for the train station.
- Peter Steiber, the innkeeper, had "served for three years at the Grosvenor Hotel in London."

- Holmes awaited Moriarty on a "three-foot path," with a sheer wall on one side and a sheer drop on the other.
- Holmes' note to Watson was written on "three pages torn from a notebook."
- Disguised as a book peddler, Holmes showed Watson three books: *British Birds, Catullus,* and *The Holy War.*
- Three deputies of Moriarty still posed a threat to Holmes after the duel at the Reichenbach Falls. "I knew," he told Watson, "that Moriarty was not the only man who had sworn my death. There were at least three others whose desire for vengeance upon me would only be increased by the death of their leader."
- Colonel Moran tried to kill Holmes as climbed the cliff at Reichenbach by hurling stones at him—three times.
- Sherlock Holmes visited three continents during the Great Hiatus: Asia, Africa and Europe.
- Watson records that Moran "was within three yards of us" in the darkened room at Camden House.
- Holmes chided Lestrade for "three undetected murders in one year."
- And, finally, Moran was the author of a book titled *Three Months in the Jungle,* an intentional contrast, surely, to Holmes' three years in exile.

In these two stories, which together constitute the heart of the Sherlockian canon, the number three is ever-present. Indeed, throughout the Sherlockian saga, three is truly a magic number. Its use is too frequent to be chance alone, and its significance is far too great to be ignored.

Deeper Shades

The Dressing-Gowns of Sherlock Holmes and the Psychology of Color

The image of Sherlock Holmes in his rooms at 221B Baker Street might include any number of familiar features—the fireplace and armchairs, the Persian slipper or violin, the jack-knifed correspondence, a gasogene, smoke drifting upward from a pipe, the table for chemical experiments, the bow window—but a mental picture of the man himself invariably has him lounging about in a dressing-gown. The attire of Holmes out-of-doors has become embedded in the popular mind (quite erroneously, of course) as a never-changing deerstalker cap and Inverness cape. The indoor Holmes, the Holmes at the top of the seventeen steps leading from Mrs. Hudson's front door, is almost as well-known (and this time quite appropriately) as the casual figure of a tall, lean gentleman in a dressing-gown and slippers.

Sherlock Holmes and the Dressing-Gown

As a respectable and essential gentleman's garment, a dressing-gown was something far more elegant than the casual bath robes that many in modern times, especially Americans, associate with the term. In the Victorian and Edwardian eras, "silk or brocade dressing or morning gowns were worn instead of a coat. They often had shawl collars, were loose fitting, wrapping over the front and were tied around the waist with a tassel ended cord."

A dressing-gown is actually defined as "a loose robe for wear when one is not fully-clothed, as before dressing or when lounging." This is an ideal description of the type of gown that Holmes wore, not only because it portrays his use of the garment perfectly, but also because of the emphasis on "not fully clothed" (which naturally implies, conversely, being either partially or mostly clothed). Unlike those who wear bath robes around the house today, Holmes never would consider relaxing in his dressing-gown with nothing (or next to nothing) underneath. The gown was a comfortable and leisurely piece of clothing, but it was worn over the trousers and shirt, replacing the man's jacket; slippers would replace the shoes.

In fourteen different cases, Watson specifically mentioned Holmes' wearing a dressing-gown. In a number of other scenes from Baker Street, the presence of a dressing-gown can be assumed. Whenever Sherlock Holmes was "lounging," he undoubtedly was doing so in his customary and comfortable dressing-gown rather than in whatever outer-wear might be appropriate for an excursion into the streets. Even so, a quick change was possible. On one occasion, at the start of his investigation in *The Valley of Fear*, Holmes agreed with Inspector MacDonald that a trip to Birlstone was in order. He "sprang up and hastened to change from his dressing-gown to his coat."

As pictured in *The Sign of Four*, Sherlock Holmes often might be found relaxed in his own home. He would turn to cocaine when he would "crave for mental exaltation," then be "leaning back luxuriously in his armchair and sending up blue wreaths from his pipe." At these times, this man was not fully dressed for the streets, the theatre or train trip. For a Victorian of Holmes' social standing, in the context of his lifestyle, such a scene hardly could find him in any sort of attire other than a dressing-gown.

The Question of the Three Gowns

Although Holmes is described in a dressing-gown on numerous occasions, the actual color is mentioned only four times: once as blue in THE MAN WITH THE TWISTED LIP, once as purple in THE BLUE CARBUNCLE, and twice as "mouse-colored" in THE EMPTY HOUSE and THE BRUCE-PARTINGTON PLANS. This seems plain enough, and many Sherlockian scholars go no further in their search for an explanation. Jack Tracy, for instance, states unequivocally that "Holmes had at least three dressing-gowns." Variations on the "three gowns theory" abound.

In his essay on the subject, S.F. Blake theorized that Holmes owned two dressing-gowns, one blue and one purple, that were ruined in the fire set by Moriarty's agents in THE FINAL PROBLEM, thus requiring Holmes to obtain another gown during his subsequent travels. This is a fanciful notion, unsupported by an solid evidence in the canon, and (in fact) demonstrably incorrect. For one thing, "no great harm was done" by the fire. Even so, this idea at least has some ring of plausibility.

On the other end of the spectrum is the "one gown only" theory. Some attribute the designation of three colors simply to Watson's inattention to detail. Father Ronald A. Knox, the originator of the higher criticism of the Holmes canon, considered the use of different gown colors as an example of "actual inconsistencies" in the text. Even worse, in an unkind and unacceptable idea, the proponents of the "drunken Watson" heresy claim that three colors are ascribed to one dressing-gown by a man whose senses were dulled by alcohol.

By far, however, the most convoluted assessment of the question was devised by Christopher Morley: "This particular own was blue when new . . . it had gone purple by the time of THE BLUE CARBUNCLE. During the long absence, 1891-94, when Mrs. Watson faithfully aired and sunned it in the back yard, it faded to mouse."

Not everyone discounts this speculation, and Judge S. Tupper Bigelow gave it his unqualified endorsement. "Sherlock Holmes perhaps had many dressing-gowns, but if we assume he had only one, the theory . . . is attractive, appealing and hardly disputable," he wrote.

However, there is plenty to dispute about such an idea and number of objections to be raised, not least of which would be the actual likelihood of cloth fading in this manner. In addition, while the good Mrs. Hudson certainly may have laundered Holmes' clothes occasionally during the Great Hiatus, a practical woman (and Mrs. Hudson certainly was practical) would not have wasted her time washing properly-stored, unworn clothing of good quality so often in only a three-year period that the color would fade on a clothes-line so dramatically.

No, Watson was an outstanding writer who knew the value of description in relating his accounts of Holmes' cases. He was also a competent professional who knew the difference between one dressing-gown and another, even if (for the sake of argument) there had been some fading to occur. His often-alleged carelessness in dates—which, in the final analysis, really does not matter in the telling of a story—was not necessarily matched with carelessness in his vivid accounts of the four scenes in which the dressing-gowns' colors are mentioned.

- Holmes perched on the cushions in the house of Neville St. Clair in THE MAN WITH THE TWISTED LIP.
- Holmes in the Christmas season, receiving his old friend's visit after what may have been a long absence, in THE BLUE CARBUNCLE.

- Holmes removing his dressing-gown from an effigy which had been shot through the head by an accomplished marksman, Colonel Sebastian Moran, in The Empty House.
- Holmes "prowling restlessly" in his rooms in The Bruce-Partington Plans.

In all four instances, Watson had good cause to remember the colors because the scenes themselves were so striking, so likely to be ingrained in his mind. That Watson gave an accurate description of the dressing-gowns and their colors is much more likely than Watson forgetting, confusing or even making-up such essential details.

There were, indeed, three dressing-gowns—one blue, one purple, and one mouse-colored. The number of gowns, their colors, their owners and origins—all of these questions have been considered several times (albeit, most often, only superficially), and the answers which have been offered are interesting enough in and of themselves. But a deeper and even more profound aspect of the three gowns also merits careful analysis. The three colors themselves—blue, purple and mouse—have great significance.

Color attracts and affects people in a variety of ways, and these three dressing-gowns were not selected for wear purely by accident or by coincidence. They were chosen by Holmes, consciously or unconsciously, specifically because of their colors; and those choices had a significant effect on the way he decided to pursue and resolve his cases. "More than anything, color has the ability to reveal a tremendous amount about a person's identity, personality, or even their sexuality." Sherlock Holmes was no exception.

The Borrowed Blue Dressing-Gown

When Sherlock Holmes agreed to assist the wife of Neville St. Clair in The Man with the Twisted Lip, he did not conduct his investigation from Baker Street. Instead, he took up quarters in the St. Clair home, The Cedars, seven miles outside of London. This arrangement, he told Watson, enabled him to pursue the "many inquiries which must be made" about St. Clair's background and personal life.

St. Clair, Watson says, "lived generally in good style." Disguised as a beggar, he had made "considerable sums of money" and "grew richer," taking a house in the country and a wife of respectable antecedents. When Holmes brought Watson to The Cedars, Mrs. St. Clair politely asked the good doctor to "forgive anything that may be wanting in our arrangements," but this was a mere formality, an expected courtesy. The house certainly was spacious and well-furnished, and all of the comforts of Victorian life were undoubtedly available. Specifically, "two rooms" were put at the disposal of Holmes and Watson, one of which was "a large and comfortable double-bedded room." The other, presumably, was an adjoining sitting-room.

After such an exciting and interesting day, Watson climbed into bed, more than ready for ready for a good night's sleep. From this vantage point, he described a highly-memorable scene:

> It was soon evident to me that [Holmes] was now preparing for an all-night sitting. He took off his coat and waistcoat, put on a large blue dressing-gown, and then wandered about the room collecting pillows from his bed and cushions from the sofa and arm-chairs. With these he constructed a sort of Eastern divan, upon which he perched himself cross-legged, with an ounce of shag tobacco and a box of matches laid-out in front of him. In the dim light of the lamp I saw him sitting there, an old briar pipe between his lips, his eyes fixed vacantly upon the corner of the ceiling, the blue smoke curling up from him, silent, motionless, with the light shining upon his strong-set aquiline features. So he was as I dropped off to sleep, and so he sat when a sudden ejaculation caused me to wake up, and I found the summer sun shining into the apartment. The pipe was still between his lips, the smoke still curled upward, and the room was full of dense tobacco haze, but nothing remained of the heap of shag which I had seen upon the previous night.

The scene inevitably calls to mind the legend of Siddhartha Gautama, the Buddha, who sat in just the sort of position assumed by Holmes for a long night of deep meditation. At dawn, his "enlightenment" came, and he knew the truth.

A man of St. Clair's means would have several dressing-gowns, probably made of silk, in his home for his own use and for the use of his guests. Martin Dakin considered the evidence and concurred with a widely-held opinion: "It has been conclusively answered that Holmes presumably did not carry his dressing-gown about with him, and that the blue one was borrowed for the occasion from St. Clair's wardrobe." Just how Mr. Dakin "conclusively" answered something that "presumably" happened is open for reasonable debate. Even so, the idea that the blue dressing-gown was borrowed from St. Clair and did not belong to Holmes is a responsible interpretation of the facts as they have been presented by Watson. Many Sherlockian scholars have concluded, rightly, that the blue dressing-gown belonged to Neville St. Clair and was provided to Holmes as part of the "arrangements" for his stay.

Regardless of who owned the blue dressing-gown, Holmes or St. Clair, it made only one appearance in the recorded history of Sherlock Holmes. During that one appearance, it had a remarkable effect on the great detective.

The Tranquil Blue of Meditation

With a choice, apparently, of dressing-gowns, Holmes selected a blue one. This may or may not have been a deliberate decision for Holmes. In other words, he may not have opened the wardrobe and said to himself, "Ah, a blue dressing-gown! Just what I needed." Even so, psychologically, his choice was natural, even necessary. According to color experts, "people often match colors to their moods," and in many instances they make "an unconscious choice."

Holmes was preparing to spend an evening in meditation and deep reflection, and the right atmosphere was essential. Blue is recognized by color psychologists and clear-eyed marketing executives alike as a color that will "promote relaxation." Morton Walker, an internationally known expert on color and its effects, asserts that "the softer hues of blue can sedate the nerves" and serve as a "quieting color." As Holmes readied himself for a most unique period of contemplation, the selection of a blue dressing-gown was an understandable and perfectly logical, if instinctive, move on his part. Holmes set the stage for his mediation by choosing the one color "known to produce a calming effect . . . the most tranquilizing color of all."

The dressing-gown was not the only blue element in the memorable scene witnessed by Watson as he drifted off to sleep in the St. Clair home. The "blue smoke" curled up from Holmes' briar pipe; and when his outburst of enlightenment awakened Watson, Holmes was still surrounded by this "dense tobacco haze." This is a literal description, but it has a symbolic interpretation as well. To be "in a fog" is to be unaware of the truth, to be groping for an explanation or looking into unknown regions. The color blue has its own significance here, since "we are conditioned to seeing distances through a bluish haze." Holmes, of course, had cut through the fog and seen past the haze. Aided in his meditation by the soothing blue color of his dressing-gown, he had solved the mystery of THE MAN WITH THE TWISTED LIP.

A Purple Gown for Christmas

Watson opened his account of THE BLUE CARBUNCLE with his second reference to Holmes' wearing a dressing-gown, this time at Baker street during the holiday season:

> I had called upon my friend Sherlock Holmes upon the second morning after Christmas, with the intention of wishing him the compliments of the season. He was lounging upon the sofa in a purple dressing-gown, a pipe rack within his reach upon the right, and a pile of morning papers, evidently newly studied, near at hand.

Rather than stating simply that Holmes was in "his dressing-gown" as he usually did (if he mentioned the gown at all), Watson made a point in this particular instance of describing the color. In all probability, the dressing-gown caught his eye and remained in his memory either because the gown was unfamiliar to him or because it was unusual and perhaps even out of character for Holmes to wear such a bold color, or both. Certainly, any writer is less likely to describe the commonplace or expected rather than the unusual or unexpected.

The color purple itself strongly implies a silk, rather than a brocade, dressing-gown; and Holmes' personality and habits would suggest that the purchase of a colorful and fairly expensive silk garment for himself would be unlikely. However, an explanation for Holmes' being in possession of a new dressing-gown is readily available. Watson's visit took place shortly after Christmas, and this circumstance would lead to the reasonable conclusion that the purple dressing-gown was a present fitting the spirit of the season.

A dressing-gown is a relatively intimate garment, worn as it is in the privacy of the home. A grateful client would be more apt to reward the master detective with money, jewelry or some other item of greater pecuniary value and more in the nature of a reward for services. So only a fairly close friend or relative would be expected to present Holmes with such a gift. However, Holmes "was never a very sociable fellow," and his only friend from college, Victor Trevor, had left the country after the affair of THE GLORIA SCOTT. Otherwise, Dr. Watson's writings provide only three credible candidates: Watson himself, Mrs. Hudson or Mycroft Holmes.

Of these three, Watson seems least likely. His own words suggest an unfamiliarity with the purple dressing-gown. Indeed, if Watson had sent the gown to Holmes, he may well have mentioned the fact when he wrote his account. Undoubtedly, he would have been pleased that Holmes thought enough of it—and of him—to wear it.

Mrs. Hudson has been suggested by others. In his often-contentious but entertaining review of the canon, Martin Dakin noted that "some commentators have maintained that, as this is the only occasion where [the dressing-gown] is described as purple, this one must have been a special Christmas present, say from Mrs. Hudson, which he was wearing in her honor and thereafter discarded." Unfortunately, Mr. Dakin dismissed the entire subject of dressing-gowns out-of-hand. However, there are very good and logical reasons to discount Mrs. Hudson's involvement.

If Mrs. Hudson were the giver, Holmes hardly would have worn the dressing-gown to please her on only one or two occasions before discarding it. After all, Mrs. Hudson saw him on a daily basis; she surely would notice that he never wore it. We learn in THE DYING DETECTIVE that Mrs. Hudson was "a long-suffering woman," but Holmes was not so insensitive that he would willfully insult her in such a manner. In addition, if she gave Holmes a Christmas present at all, Mrs. Hudson would not be inclined to give him something so personal. An item that would help control his state of order in her otherwise orderly house would be more plausible. After all, "his incredible untidiness" and other bad habits "made him the very worst tenant in London."

Therefore, the process of elimination leaves brother Mycroft. He would face no obstacle because of the intimate nature of the gift, and the gift itself would fit Mycroft's own personality. Mycroft Holmes was a large, lethargic man who had little energy and refused to take exercise beyond his normal daily routine. "Heavily built and massive, there was a suggestion of uncouth physical inertia in the figure." But the real clue to the dressing-gown can be found in Watson's description of Mycroft's eyes, which "seemed to always retain that far-away, introspective look which I had only observed in Sherlock's when he was exerting his full powers."

The Holmes brothers were as similar intellectually as they were different physically. Just as Mrs. Hudson would give Sherlock Holmes a practical gift for the sake of her household, so would Mycroft present him with a thinking-friendly gift for the sake of his mind. Mycroft would want to facilitate his brother's introspection, to allow him to be indolent in body while active in mind, just as he, himself, was prone to be. No better facilitator, no better gift, could be found than a high-quality, silk dressing-gown for Sherlock's periods of lounging in the comfort of his rooms on Baker Street.

The Authority of Purple

Nowhere in the history of Sherlock Holmes did the psychology of color have as great an effect on the master detective as in THE BLUE CARBUNCLE. The purple dressing-gown took hold in Holmes' unconscious mind and allowed him to reach a height of presumption to which he never again aspired.

An understanding of why this is true requires an understanding of the significance of the color purple, or violet, in the two thousand years prior to, and including, the Victorian age. "The purple robe or mantle has long been a symbol of royalty and spiritual authority." Holmes' treatment of James Ryder quite clearly was influenced by the dual authorities associated with the color purple: the authority of the crown and the authority of the church.

Purple clothing was once very costly to produce because the dye was so difficult to keep colorfast; and, as a result, the color became the symbol of royalty. The very phrase "born to the purple" describes an individual of royal or high birth; and, in some societies, the wearing of purple was the exclusive right of the royal family. This connection between the purple and the imperial is an ancient one, and the earliest stories of the Bible mention "the purple garments worn by the kings of Midian" (Judges 8:26). Purple "is associated with the Roman monarchy because the Emperor's state robes were of purple. The color became almost a synonym for the throne."

Incidentally, the selection of a purple-colored dressing-gown as a Christmas present for Sherlock Holmes further points to his brother Mycroft as the giver. Mycroft Holmes was in service to the crown, as regal concerns were never far from his thoughts. The psychology of color would have its effect on Mycroft, just as it did on Sherlock or Watson.

As a symbol of religious authority, the purple vestment recalls the Passion of Christ and his own royal stature, as recorded in Mark 15:16-20:

> Then the soldiers led him into the courtyard of the palace . . . And they clothed him in a purple cloak; and after twisting some thorns into a crown, they put it on him. And they began saluting him, "Hail, King of the Jews!" They struck his head with a reed, spat upon him, and knelt down in homage to him. After mocking him, they stripped him of the purple cloak and put his own clothes on him. Then they led him out to crucify him.

Because of this, in the Roman Catholic Church, "purple or violet vestments are worn on days of intercession, and for several ecclesiastical functions, especially those concerned with the Passion." In addition, purple "is the official liturgical color for the season of Advent," a four-week season that centers on the coming of Christ and culminates on Christmas Eve in "anticipation of the celebration of his Nativity." When Watson visited Sherlock Holmes, Advent was barely completed, and no color could have connected as well with the authority of the Church in that season as did purple.

The Power of Purple

Experts in color psychology well understand the effect that purple can have on individuals who wear it. Says Morton Walker: "In its negative aspect, violet can overwhelm a person unprepared for the snobbery, pretense and even deceit can generate."

The power of purple is demonstrated not only in the color itself, but more specifically in purple clothing: the purple cloaks of royalty, the purple vestments of the clergy, the purple dressing-gown of Sherlock Holmes. In THE BLUE CARBUNCLE, Holmes—perhaps unconsciously—merged these three into one and became, all at once, detective and priest and king.

Holmes presumed to take on these roles at the end of the case, when, after breaking down James Ryder and forcing him to admit his guilt, Holmes "threw open the door" and allowed the felon to flee. He rationalized this action to an undoubtedly astonished Watson: "After all, Watson . . . I am not retained by the police to supply their deficiencies . . . I suppose that I am commuting a felony, but it is just possible that I am saving a soul."

Sherlockian scholars with a legal background recognized long ago that "commuting a felony" was an action well outside the authority not only of a common citizen such as Sherlock Holmes, but indeed was forbidden to anyone in Britain other than the monarch. In a scholarly brief in *The Baker Street Journal*, a British counsel identified only as "E.J.C." doubted that an Englishman would "presume to so use the word." He argued:

> [The law] provides, among other things, that the power to pardon an offense, or *commute* or reduce or remit the punishment or fine for a criminal offense is a *prerogative of the Crown* and may not be delegated *to a subject* . . . I apprehend that . . . no Englishman willingly invades the prerogative of the Sovereign or presumes to exercise a non-delegable power.

Notwithstanding this declaration, and even though Sherlock Holmes possessed "a good practical knowledge of British law," he did, indeed, presume to exercise that power. William S. Baring-Gould wondered if the whole episode revealed that Holmes "had royal blood in his veins."

The question of Holmes' nationality really is not relevant. Even so, the evidence seems overwhelming that, despite some high-profile contentions to the contrary, Holmes was an unusually loyal Englishman who thought so highly of his Queen that he embedded her initials—"a patriotic V.R."—by pistol-shot into the wall of his sitting-room in THE MUSGRAVE RITUAL. Certainly, no American would be obliged to feel particularly "patriotic" about an English queen.

"Saving a soul," of course, is a patently religious reference, and its use by Holmes "recalls the absolution offered by a Roman Catholic priest after confession." Now, Holmes was not above impersonating a "venerable Italian priest" for purposes of disguise, as he did in THE FINAL PROBLEM. However, there is no evidence that he attempted to perform any of the sacraments while masquerading in this way.

Of course, assuming that Holmes was taking on he authority of a priest is the best case scenario. Catholic doctrine clearly states that "salvation comes from God alone," a belief shared by Protestants of all denominations. Yet, Sherlock Holmes dared claim the capacity to save a soul for himself. There is no question of Holmes' vanity; he demonstrated that trait on many occasions. Moreover, many a student of the canon has suggested that he was at least an agnostic, if not an atheist. But claiming the power of God himself seems to be over the line, even for someone, like Holmes, with a powerful ego.

There can be no dispute about the facts. Holmes assumed powers he did not rightly possess. One of those powers, "commuting a felony, belonged to the Queen (or King) alone. The other, "saving a soul," was rightfully exercised by God, or at least by his duly ordained priests. In both cases, the presumption was out of character for Holmes, a one-time-only trespass into forbidden regions. What made this case different was the presence of that purple garment, the color of which was linked solidly in the recesses of every Victorian mind with the authority of royalty and of the church.

Perhaps Holmes recognized the dangerous influence of the purple dressing-gown. It is not difficult to envision him in his rooms, thoughtfully folding his garment, putting it away as a souvenir of an exceptional case, and resolving to avoid its temptations in the future. Indeed, never again was Holmes known to wear that purple dressing-gown, and never again did he dare step into the shoes of sovereign monarchs of either the British Empire or the Universe itself.

One Gown Was Quite Enough

Neither Neville St. Clair's blue dressing-gown nor the ultimately unsuitable purple dressing-gown was destined to become the garment of choice for Sherlock Holmes. However, Watson notes in *A Study in Scarlet* that "his habits were regular," and the idea that Holmes had a trunk full of dressing-gowns seems very much out of character. No less an authority than Michael Harrison had this to say about the nature of the Holmes wardrobe:

> I think I may venture to affirm, from all that I have seen and read of Mr. Holmes, that his wardrobe grew, piece by essential piece, from the scantily indispensable kit of an impecunious para-medical student to the super-extensive wardrobe of his established Baker Street practice, always by deliberate need-imposed choice—and that vanity entered into that continuous wardrobe-expansion not at all.

A fairly extensive selection of clothing was necessary for Holmes. After all, he had to keep up with all of the expectations attached to a person of his social class. He was required to appear in any number of settings, formal and informal, in the course of his investigations. He attended the theatre and other places for functions at which proper dress would be required. And he was generally successful financially, permitting him to purchase whatever clothing he might reasonable want or require. In addition, he needed a variety of garments for his many disguises.

Even so, such a collection was necessary for public rather than private use. Being a creature of habit in so many ways, Holmes probably desired no more than one dressing-gown. Certainly, there was no cause for a "need-imposed choice" of more than one. In apparent contradiction to his own conclusions, Harrison estimated that Holmes would have "4 dressing-gowns, various cloths" in 1895. This seems very unlikely. Without some essential need—and considering carefully all of the references available relating to Holmes' dressing-gowns—the master detective almost certainly wore only one dressing-gown, a comfortable and reliable mouse-colored garment which suited him and his moods more than adequately and which he saw no need whatsoever to replace.

The One True Dressing-Gown

The account of Colonel Moran's attempted assassination of Sherlock Holmes in THE EMPTY HOUSE substantiates the theory that Holmes had one, and only one, dressing-gown. Watson related that Moran, hiding in Camden House across from Holmes' rooms, shot at "a wax colored model of my friend, so admirably done that it was a perfect facsimile. It stood on a small pedestal table with an old dressing-gown of Holmes' so draped round it that the illusion from the street was absolutely perfect." This particular reference, taken alone, proves nothing since "an old dressing-gown" is imprecise and ambiguous without proper context. That context, however, is readily available. Only moments later, Watson revealed in very clear terms the truth about the dressing-gown: Holmes "had thrown off the seedy frockcoat, and now he was the Holmes of old in the mouse-colored dressing-gown which he took from his effigy."

Three essential points can be gleaned from these important passages in the account of Holmes' return. First, the mouse-colored dressing-gown was "old" and had belonged to Holmes in years gone by (thus disproving S.F. Blake's theory that it was purchased during the Great Hiatus). Second, the effigy was a "perfect facsimile" of Holmes, and the mouse-colored dressing-gown was necessary to make it perfect. Holmes was known to wear that gown in his Baker Street rooms; no disguise would succeed without it.

Third, and most important, Holmes was suddenly fully recognizable to Watson—and the reality of the detective's dramatic return to life was fully appreciated by his faithful friend—only after he put on the mouse-colored dressing-gown and became "the Holmes of old." All of Watson's disbelief, all of his numbness, all of his shock, all of any doubt about his own senses he may have felt—all melted away when he saw Sherlock Holmes in that particular gown in that particular place. That this gown had such a dramatic effect on Watson, that "the Holmes of old" was incomplete without a mouse-colored dressing-gown, prove almost conclusively that this garment, and this garment alone, was Sherlock Holmes' one-and-only, exclusively preferred dressing-gown. It was "his dressing-gown."

This phrase, "his dressing-gown," is no simple descriptive device. Other than the four instances in which a specific color described a dressing-gown worn by Holmes (once blue, once purple and twice mouse-colored), a possessive pronoun was used in every single case when this garment was mentioned. In six adventures occurring prior to the Great Hiatus and the very exciting events described in THE EMPTY HOUSE, Watson employed this term. In another, Holmes himself is quoted as referring to "my dressing-gown."

A review of those seven instances (emphasis added) in roughly chronological order would illustrate the point:

- THE BERYL CORONET: "My friend rose lazily from his armchair and stood with his hands in the pockets of *his dressing-gown* looking over my shoulder."
- THE RESIDENT PATIENT: "At half past seven next morning, in the first dim glimmer of daylight, I found him standing by my bedside in *his dressing-gown*."
- THE VALLEY OF FEAR: "Holmes ... sprang up and hastened to change from *his dressing-gown* to his coat."
- THE NAVAL TREATY: "Holmes was seated at his side-table clad in *his dressing-gown* and working hard over a chemical investigation."
- THE CARDBOARD BOX: "I'll be back in a moment when I have changed *my dressing-gown* and filled my cigar case."
- THE ENGINEER'S THUMB: "Sherlock Holmes was, as I expected, lounging about his sitting-room in *his dressing-gown* reading the agony column of *The Times* and smoking his before-breakfast pipe ..."
- THE HOUND OF THE BASKERVILLES: "Through the haze I had a vague vision of Holmes in *his dressing-gown* coiled up in an armchair with his black clay pipe between his lips" (Chapter 3). Also: "Our breakfast-table was cleared early, and Holmes waited in *his dressing-gown* for the promised interview" (Chapter 4).

One other specific mention of the dressing-gown was made prior to the Great Hiatus. During the dramatic confrontation between Holmes and Moriarty in the rooms at Baker Street as recorded in THE FINAL PROBLEM, the evil professor noticed that the master detective had a revolver in his pocket. Commented Moriarty: "It is a dangerous habit to finger loaded firearms in the pocket of one's dressing-gown." Now, Moriarty possessed a superior intellect. His powers of observation surpassed those of most people, and they may even have been comparable to those of Sherlock Holmes. Interestingly enough, he also used a possessive pronoun ("one's") to describe the dressing-gown.

Clearly, to the quick eye of Professor Moriarty, this garment was familiar and comfortable to Holmes. It was his customary apparel at home, "his" dressing-gown. When Moriarty departed, he took this knowledge with him and can confidently be expected to have passed it on to his minions. No wonder, then, that the deception of Colonel Moran by using the wax model was so successful. Moran knew to look for this particular dressing-gown when he tried to assassinate Holmes from the window of Camden House.

The attempt to identify the one true dressing-gown of Sherlock Holmes hinges on the account of THE EMPTY HOUSE in the context of this and all previous mentions of this garment. Up to the time of the Great Hiatus, Holmes had worn a blue dressing-gown once, a purple dressing-gown once, and "his" dressing-gown many times. Watson clearly identified the mouse-colored gown as "old" and as the habitual clothing of "the Holmes of old." Because of this, all of those references to "his" or "my" or "one's" dressing-gown could not have referred to either the purple or the blue garment. The mouse-colored dressing-gown and "his" dressing-gown were one and the same.

Gray versus Mouse

At the beginning of THE DANCING MEN, Watson stated that Holmes "looked from my point of view like a strange, lank bird, with dull gray plumage and a black top-knot." The allusion to "gray plumage" was indirect, but it almost certainly was a reference to the mouse-colored dressing-gown. However, there is a very important difference in this instance. Here, the color reference was actually to a hypothetical bird, not to the dressing-gown. "Mouse-colored" would be an inappropriate description of a bird; Watson reserved that term for the dressing-gown when it was worn by his friend.

Perhaps a case can be made that gray would have served Watson's descriptive purposes just as well. Gray has its own connotations for color psychologists. According to Morton Walker, "The simplest color for the eye to process is gray. It . . . inspires creativity, enhances artistic appreciation and symbolizes success." Holmes certainly possessed all three of these qualities: creativity in his own approach to the art of detection, artistic appreciation (especially of music), and success unparalleled in his field. If these were the psychological impacts of gray, he certainly benefited from the subconscious effects that the color produced.

On the other hand, gray has undertones of meaning that under no circumstances would apply to Sherlock Holmes. A "gray area" is a vague zone between morality and immorality or between legality and illegality. Color experts classify gray as a "weak" color, as opposed to "strong" or "bold" colors that produce more or less predictable psychological effects. Some marketing professionals look upon gray as "the color preferred by people who are indecisive." Vagueness, weakness and indecisiveness were alien to the nature of Sherlock Holmes, and the dressing-gown clearly did not produce those qualities in him, even temporarily.

So there must have been more to the dressing-gown than the usual associations that have been established for gray. In Sherlock Holmes, the mouse-colored dressing-gown produced a certain degree of agitation, a call to action, a desire to prowl. The reason for this must lie, not in the grayness of the dressing-gown, but in the unusual word that was selected to describe it: "mouse." Holmes must not have thought of his dressing-gown as gray, even subconsciously; he thought of it as mouse-colored.

Unlike blue or purple, the word "mouse" is not commonly used to describe a color. A mouse, after all, is an animal. As a color, it is commonly defined as "dark gray with a yellowish tinge." Watson, like Holmes, certainly recognized the actual color involved, and he presumably would have used the word "gray" if it had the connotation for Holmes that he wanted to convey. Quite apparently, it did not.

The Prowling Gown

Once resettled at Baker Street, with Moran safely out of the picture, Holmes returned to his old ways and to his old dressing-gown. There can be little doubt that for the remainder of his career as a consulting detective, he held onto the mouse-colored dressing-gown that suited him so well, although it was specifically mentioned only three more times.

In THE MAZARIN STONE, the dressing-gown figured in two familiar scenarios. In a reprise of his trick upon Colonel Moran in THE EMPTY HOUSE, he used a dummy, "dressing-gown and all," to deceive Count Sylvius and his agents. In the same story, in a scene reminiscent of Moriarty's visit, "Holmes held something protruding from the pocket of his dressing-gown"—a pistol, of course, held at the ready for any violence that Sylvius might attempt.

Incidentally, the story of THE MAZARIN STONE opens the possibility that Holmes had a second dressing-gown, one for the wax dummy and another, his habitual dressing-gown, for himself. Switching places with the dummy required stealth and finesse enough without Holmes' having to undress it as well. Count Sylvius and Sam Merton might have noticed that much activity. However, the dummy's dressing-gown would necessarily have to be exactly the same as the one Holmes was wearing. In other words, if Holmes did obtain a second dressing-gown for this ruse, it was also a mouse-colored one. So the idea that he used only one dressing-gown, that being a mouse-colored gown, stands.

The details of THE MAZARIN STONE are interesting enough, but the other two appearances of the dressing-gown in the post-Hiatus adventures are more important since they provide the clues which help solve the meaning and significance attached to Holmes' choice of a "mouse-colored" gown for his habitual wear. Watson provided this striking account of an agitated Sherlock Holmes attempting to discover the whereabouts of Lady Frances Carfax:

> Sherlock Holmes was too irritable for conversation and too restless for sleep. I left him smoking hard, with his heavy, dark brows knotted together, and his long, nervous fingers tapping upon the arms of his chair, as he turned over in his mind every possible solution to the mystery. Several times in the course of the night I heard him prowling about the house. Finally, just after I had been called in the morning, he rushed into my room. He was in his dressing-gown, but his pale, hollow-eyed face told me that his night had been a sleepless one.

The comparison between this spectacle and the much more tranquil scene described in THE MAN WITH THE TWISTED LIP bears close examination. On one hand several similarities deserve to be noted: a difficult mystery, an all-night pondering of the case, the stimulus of tobacco, the wearing of a dressing-gown, Watson blissfully sleeping through the whole thing. Yet the entire tenor of the overnight vigil was completely different, and it must be highly significant that the descriptions of Holmes himself and his behavior could not be more dissimilar.

THE MAN WITH THE TWISTED LIP	THE DISAPPEARANCE OF LADY FRANCES CARFAX
perched cross legged	restless
tobacco and a box of matches laid out in front of him	smoking hard
eyes fixed vacantly	heavy, dark brows knotted together
silent	nervous fingers tapping
motionless	prowling about
light shining upon his strong-set aquiline features	irritable
eyes twinkled	hollow-eyed
so he sat when a sudden ejaculation caused me to wake up	he rushed into my room

For most men, knowledge of the virtues of thoughtfulness, relaxation and reflection come later in life. Yet Holmes, many years after his success with the oriental-style meditation in St. Clair's house, seems to have regressed rather than progressed in his methods. The situation, the personal needs, the setting, the time of day, even the companionship of Watson were all comparable. Therefore, one might expect Holmes to return to the approach that had worked so admirably at least once before. Instead, he was tremendously agitated.

The explanation for this phenomenon must rest in an element that was very different from that scene at The Cedars. One such element comes to mind. The dressing-gown that he wore in the earlier case was blue, the color of relaxation. The dressing-gown of his later years was mouse-colored—a color that clearly produced a very different psychological effect upon its wearer.

This extraordinary effect was also plainly evident in Watson's description of Holmes' behavior during THE BRUCE-PARTINGTON PLANS:

> His eager face still wore that expression of intense and high-strung energy, which showed me that some novel and suggestive circumstance had opened up a stimulating line of thought. See the foxhound with hanging ears and drooping tail as it lolls around the kennels, and compare it with the same hound as, with gleaming eyes and straining muscles, it runs upon a breast-high scent—such was the change in Holmes since the morning. He was a different man from the limp and lounging figure in the mouse-colored dressing-gown who had prowled so restlessly only a few hours before round the fog-girt room.

The sense of agitation prevails in this account, too; and there is a common word in both. In one, he was "prowling about the house." In the other, he "prowled . . . round the fog-girt room." So the mouse-colored dressing-gown continued to be Holmes' gown of choice, and it—like the other gowns—had a conspicuous effect on him. Clearly, it was a dressing-gown that incited him to action. It was his "prowling gown."

Man and Mouse

At first glance, comparing Sherlock Holmes to a mouse seems ridiculous, and rightly so. In Watson's time as today, to call any man a "mouse" was an insult, since mice are usually depicted as timid or weak, the prey rather than the predator. Homes was none of these. Neither friend nor foe of the master detective believed for a moment that he was anything less than courageous and self-confident, strong in both body and force of personality. No need to ask the time-worn question of Sherlock Holmes: He was a man, not a mouse.

So any attempt to connect the mouse-colored dressing-gown with the animal of that name must fail because the psychological connection fails so utterly. However, "mouse" has another meaning. That meaning is infinitely more apt for application to the great Sherlock Holmes—and that meaning explains why this dressing-gown was also Holmes' "prowling gown." The following definitions of the verb "mouse" from *The Oxford English Dictionary* (emphasis added) appear to be more than pertinent and help explain both of what was in Watson's mind and what effect the dressing-gown had on Holmes:

> The hunt or search industriously or captiously; to go or move about softly in search of something, *to prowl*... To hunt for by patient and careful search.

The implications for Sherlock Holmes are obvious. His entire personality, his methods of detection, his approach to any case—all are reflected in this dictionary definition. There is no need to chronicle Holmes' ability to "move about softly," his many diligent searches, his patient and careful methods as he probed for facts. Virtually every account of his investigations is replete with pertinent references, and anyone familiar with the master detective would have no trouble envisioning Sherlock Holmes as a "mouser."

A "mouser," of course, most often (but not always) refers to a cat, and Watson had occasion to make such a comparison when describing Holmes. In *The Valley of Fear*, Watson noted "one of his quick feline pounces," suggesting that this classic description of a "mouser" was a matter of course for Sherlock Holmes. The good doctor also spoke in *The Hound of the Baskervilles* of "the catlike love of personal cleanliness which is one of his characteristics."

In a broader sense, though, another animal conveyed the hunting and searching aspects of "Holmes the mouser" more clearly than even the cat. In his account of THE BRUCE-PARTINGTON PLANS (previously cited), Watson made a direct connection between Sherlock Holmes, the foxhound, and the mouse-colored dressing-gown. This was no one-time notion for Watson. The comparison of Holmes to this first-rate hunting dog had made its appearance very early in the canon. As Watson watched Holmes operate in *A Study in Scarlet*, he "was irresistibly reminded of a pure-blooded, well-trained foxhound, as it dashes backward and forward through he covert, wining in its eagerness, until it comes across a lost scent."

Years later, the comparison still held. In THE DEVIL'S FOOT, Watson described a hyperactive Holmes "out on the lawn, in through the window, round the room, for all the world like a dashing foxhound drawing a cover." Holmes played the role of "mouser" throughout his career.

The mouse-color of Sherlock Holmes' favorite dressing-gown had an effect on both the wearer (Holmes) and the observer (Watson). That effect certainly was not to associate "mouse-colored" with the timidity or meekness of the mouse. The obvious will not serve in this instance. Instead, the psychological connection was with the act of "mousing," of searching and investigating every possible nook and cranny. Watson, more than likely in an subconscious way, recognized this implication and used the term "mouse-colored" rather than "gray." Holmes, himself, clearly was moved by the impact of the color of the dressing-gown as he pursued his solutions to the oft-perplexing problems that came his way. He was the "mouser," drawing on the ancient skills found in the creatures of nature to snare his prey.

Conclusion

The human mind is a complex thing. Its workings are mysterious, its channels are largely uncharted, and its methods are shrouded in obscurity. Professionals in the field of psychology have learned through painstaking observation that color can have a tangible effect on behavior and attitudes. Sometimes that effect is subtle; less often, it can be profound. This discovery has a wide range of implications for society, from therapy for the seriously mentally ill to profitability for fast-food restaurant owners.

Despite being a medical professional, Dr. John H. Watson, writing as he did in the Victorian era, probably knew nothing of color psychology. His observations of Sherlock Holmes were biographical in nature and entertaining in intent. Yet, the clues he provided through the three dressing-gowns validate the modern psychologist's conclusions about the effects of color, even upon such a strong personality as that of Sherlock Holmes.

Watson provided a glimpse of the meditative Holmes of the blue dressing-gown, the imperious Holmes of the purple dressing-gown, and the constantly inquisitive Holmes of the mouse-colored dressing-gown—three essential aspects in the personality of an individual who has captured the imagination of generations and inspired the kind of analysis that few other characters in fact or fiction have undergone.

From the time that "the scarlet thread of murder" appeared in his first recorded case, Sherlock Holmes lived in a world of often-vivid colors. Perhaps, someday, if *The Whole Art of Detection* finally makes its way into print, Holmes can draw from his first-hand experiences with three common dressing-gowns to describe how color can affect the workings of the human mind.

Leading with the Chin

Careful Considerations Concerning Canonical Chins

Sherlock Holmes is described in detail throughout the canon, but his chin—though frequently mentioned—is mentioned only sparingly. He was, by habit, clean shaven, since he kept his chin "smooth," whether "in Baker Street" or upon the desolate moor (*The Hound of the Baskervilles*, Chapter 12). More notably, Watson observed that Holmes' chin "had the prominence and squareness which mark the man of determination" (*A Study in Scarlet*, Chapter 2).

The idea that physical characteristics reflected personality traits was a common thread in the Sherlockian saga. For instance, we learn in THE BLUE CARBUNCLE that Holmes himself believed that intelligence was nothing more than "a question of cubic capacity." Such a notion is not well-accepted these days. Most of us in the 21st Century accept the argument that physical characteristics are the product of genetics, while psychological and/or behavioral factors are the result of social and environmental influences. An educated person would be hard-pressed to agree with an assertion that someone with eyes set close together is probably either stupid or a criminal.

Dr. Watson, however, was free of such ideas. For him, Holmes had a chin which exposed him as a "man of determination." Specifically, his chin was prominent and square. Chin-wise, only one other character is described in these terms. Birdy Edwards had "a remarkable face," which featured "a square projecting chin" (*The Valley of Fear*, Chapter 7).

That such an admirable and heroic a person as Edwards had the canonical chin most like Holmes' should come as no surprise. But what of Jonathan Small—conspirator, murderer, thief, fugitive—who possessed "a singular prominence about his bearded chin which marked a man who was not easily turned from him purpose" (*The Sign of Four*, Chapter 11). Small, then, was also a "man of determination," but he was certainly no Sherlock Holmes or Birdy Edwards. He was on the other side of the law—he was a bad guy. Why didn't his chin make the difference?

Well, Small's chin was prominent, but apparently not square. Perhaps, had his chin possessed squareness as well as prominence, he might have taken a different path in life; he might have been able to outwit the Sikhs at the Agra fort; he might even have had enough sense not to swim with crocodiles in the Ganges. Alas, however, his chin met only one of the two standards-of-excellence-for-chins in the Sherlockian canon. The chin of Jonathan Small was only half good enough.

Others possessed chins that spoke volumes about their owners' character. The King of Bohemia is particularly notable. He had "a long straight chin suggestive of resolution pushed to the length of obstinacy" (A SCANDAL IN BOHEMIA). Jonathan Small, already mentioned, had an "aggressive chin." Such a description, on one hand, begs explanation. But it also conjures up a vision of the man wagging his beard in the face of a startled merchant or barrister as he bellowed his indignation or pressed his demands.

The Feminine Chin

The faces of women, too, featured chins which reflected personality, usually favorably. The noblewoman who revenged herself upon the odious blackmailer, Charles Augustus Milverton, made a positive impression upon Dr. Watson: "I looked at that delicately curved nose, at the marked eyebrows, at the straight mouth, and the strong little chin beneath it" (CHARLES AUGUSTUS MILVERTON). And a strong character she was indeed—strong enough to pump "bullet after bullet into Milverton's shrinking body."

Sherlock Holmes was successful in producing an extremely accurate description of Anna Coram of THE GOLDEN PINCE-NEZ purely through deduction, but he did not predict her "long and obstinate chin." Despite a long list of Anna's unattractive characteristics, Watson detected "a gallantry in the defiant chin and in the upraised head, which compelled something of respect and determination."

Finally, Eugenia Ronder kept most of her face covered by a thick dark veil, "but it was cut off close at her upper lip and disclosed a perfectly shaped mouth and a delicately rounded chin. I could conceive that she had indeed been a very remarkable woman," Watson noted in THE VEILED LODGER. Apparently, then, when all else failed, the right kind of chin could redeem an otherwise hopeless character.

The Three Little Pigs

As we all know, the Big Bad Wolf wanted to eat up the Three Little Pigs. There were other tasty creatures about, of course, and they might have been easier to get than pigs who were clever enough to build houses. But, no, the wolf wanted pigs; and the reason for that is found in this classic exchange:

"Little pig, little pig, let me come in."
"No, no, by the hair of my chinny, chin, chin."

The pigs, you see, were fat. Good eating for voracious wolves in fairy tale forests. They were so fat, in fact, that they had three chins each—thus, the "chinny, chin, chin" rather than just "chin."

Holmes and Watson encountered characters with multiple chins as well—and it just so happens that these corpulent personages numbered exactly three. The "Three Little Pigs" of the Sherlockian tales were not so little, really, but they were all noteworthy because of their chins.

Take the loathsome Jephro Rucastle, master of THE COPPER BEECHES for example. He was "a prodigiously stout man with a very smiling face, and a great heavy chin which rolled down in fold upon fold over his throat." Violent Hunter described him as "genial" and very funny, the only stand-up comic in the canon, and the very picture of the stereotypical fat man who also must be jolly. Rucastle calls to mind the fat fellows who entertained Julius Caesar. "Let me have men about me that are fat!" demanded Caesar (at least according to Shakespeare), and he might have liked jolly old Jephro very much—although it's hard to imagine that Rucastle would not have joined in the bloodletting on that ancient Ides of March.

Then there is the case of Culverton Smith, a man who murdered his own nephew and tried to do the same to Sherlock Holmes in THE DYING DETECTIVE. He possessed "a great yellow face, coarse grained and greasy, with heavy, double-chin." He could be pleasant, though certainly not jolly, but this double-chinned fellow was just as odious as Rucastle.

The last of the canonical porkers is Dr. Thorneycroft Huxtable of THE PRIORY SCHOOL. Watson recalled the "sudden and startling" entrance of Dr. Huxtable into the Baker Street rooms, his collapse, and his recovery (due in part to milk and biscuits). Then follows a truly remarkable paragraph, quoting Holmes:

"And now, Dr. Huxtable, when you have consumed that milk, you will kindly tell me what has happened, when it happened, how it happened, and, finally, what Dr. Thorneycroft Huxtable, of the priory School near Mackleton, has to do with the matter, and why he comes three days after the event—the state of your chin gives the date—to ask for my humble services."

Now, there is much to comment upon here; but the most interesting aspect of this statement is the observation by Holmes on the state of Huxtable's chin. Holmes, merely by looking at him, gives a date of three days since whatever terrible event had occurred (at that point in the narrative, unknown) to drive him, eventually, to Holmes' door. Watson himself had noticed that "the rolling chins were unshaven"—another fat, many-chinned character—but Holmes not only noticed that fact (as he would, of course, in an instant), he also determined that Huxtable had not shaved for three days. Not "about" three days, nor "approximately" three days, nor "three days or so"—exactly three days.

Watson often wanted to know just how Holmes seemed to "know" things, and this is one instance where an explanation would be welcome. Different people have different patterns of beard growth. A dark, heavily bearded man might look unshaven by nightfall, while another might have a very slow growth of the beard and days may go by before it is noticeable. All of this has something to do with hormones, and stress, and natural beard heaviness, and (ultimately) genetics, and perhaps even the humidity and altitude. Perhaps beard growth was one of Holmes' fields of "out-of-the-way knowledge which would astonish his professors" (*A Study in Scarlet*, Chapter 1), and he knew exactly how those numerous chins would appear only three days after the last good shave.

Keeping Chins Handy

Chins, unlike hands, are difficult to maneuver. What, after all, can you do with a chin? Hands are different. What mother has not demanded of her child, "Get your hands out of your mouth!"—especially if nail-biting is involved. Fathers understand, if they cannot condone, the over-use of hands by sons passing through the portals of pubescence. The strumming of fingers is annoying; the picking of noses is disgusting; and everyone knows where bumbling bureaucrats keep their thumbs most of the time.

Yes, one has to be careful about where hands are kept. But there is one place for hands that is almost always safe and rarely, if ever, offensive—the chin. Ask an actor to strike a "thoughtful" pose, and he is most likely to grasp chin between finger and thumb and assume a look of deepest concentration. No wonder, then, that chins are found in hands throughout the canon. There was even one collective chin-holding, when Holmes, Watson and Mary Morstan called on Thaddeus Sholto: "We sat all three in a semi-circle, with our heads advanced and our chins upon our hands" (*The Sign of Four*, Chapter 4).

On many other occasions, Holmes proved to be an accomplished chin-holder. This was, quite apparently, tremendously beneficial to concentration and deep thinking. Once, Watson described how "Holmes sat down on a boulder and rested his chin in his hands. I smoked two cigarettes before he moved" (THE PRIORY SCHOOL). At another time, Holmes "sat silent now for some time, with his chin upon his hand, lost in thought" (THE YELLOW FACE). But his best use of chin holding was during his visit to Devonshire: "Holmes took the bag, and descending into the hollow, he pushed the matting into a more central position. Then stretching himself upon his face and leaning his chin upon his hands, he made a careful study of the trampled mud in front of him" (SILVER BLAZE).

This chin-in-hand business must have been the exclusive province of investigators. Inspector Alec MacDonald "sat with his chin in his hands" when consulting Sherlock Holmes (*The Valley of Fear*, Chapter 2); and Inspector Bardle of Sussex "rubbed his chin" as he considered the facts in the death of Fitzroy McPherson in THE LION'S MANE. Chin-holding in Victorian times was good, clean fun.

Get It Off Your Chest

For all his chin-grasping, which is common enough even today, Holmes had another chin related practice. He would, from time to time, place it "upon his breast." Sherlock Holmes was a top-flight thinker, and breast-resting the chin apparently was the next step up on the pondering scale. There are four examples of this unusual phenomenon, all involving a different degree of associated activity, from lethargic to highly energetic. Interestingly, in three of these four examples, Holmes' hands were kept in his pockets—thus removing that temptation from the equation.

To get the highest possible level of concentration, the chin was kept tightly on the chest and distractions were kept to a minimum. In CHARLES AUGUSTUS MILVERTON, "Holmes sat motionless by the fire, his hands buried deep in his trouser pockets, his chin sunk upon his breast, his eyes fixed upon the glowing embers." Another low-energy example occurred in THE STOCKBROKER'S CLERK, when "Holmes stood by the table with his hands deep in his trouser pockets and his chin upon his breast."

Such languid approaches were not always appropriate, however. "For a whole day my companion had rambled about the room with his chin upon his chest and his brows knitted, charging and recharging his pipe with the strongest black tobacco, and absolutely deaf to any of my questions or remarks," Watson reports in SILVER BLAZE. Holmes clearly was able to be in constant motion and in deepest thought simultaneously—but the chin had to be deeply implanted in the chest to make it work.

The last example of this method demands attention. "We found Holmes," says Watson in THE REIGATE SQUIRES, "pacing up and down in the field, his chin sunk upon his breast, and his hands thrust in his trousers pockets." Now, Holmes walking around in his own apartment holding his chin down on his chest might be possible (see the previous example), since he knew the layout of the place intimately and he could be expected not to fall over the footstool *a la* Dick Van Dyke. But out in a field? I tried this in my back yard, and you can be sure that "pacing up and down" is pretty difficult if your chin is down on your breast. While I managed not to pace my way into the creek, I also discovered a hole in the ground, nearly fell over a tough clump of grass, found my dog's latest contribution to the fertilization cycle, and otherwise scared myself. Pacing will work, and butting the chin on the chest will work, but both at the same time? Well, we know Holmes could do it, but lesser mortals would have a more challenging time.

The Chin Grotesque

Not all chins in the world of Sherlock Holmes were fun to observe. Hugh Boone, the alter ego of Neville St. Clair, took pains to make himself ugly as the principal character in THE MAN WITH THE TWISTED LIP. He possessed "a bulldog chin," and his disguise included "an old scar . . . from eye to chin."

Sometimes, the chins could take on a ghastly aspect. In the same story, Watson described the scene in an opium den on Upper Swandam Lane: "Through the gloom one could dimly catch a glimpse of bodies lying in strange fantastic poses, bowed shoulders, bent knees, heads thrown back, and chins pointing upward." The chins of the opium addicts apparently were like tulips in a Dutch garden, straining upward and ready to be plucked.

Even more macabre is the scene in the "haunted crypt" of SHOSCOMBE OLD PLACE, when Holmes confronted Sir Robert Norberton. "He turned and tore open the coffin-lid behind him. In the glare of the lantern I saw a body swathed in a sheet form head to foot, with dreadful, witch-like features, all nose and chin, projecting at one end, the dim, glazed eyes staring from a discolored and crumbling face." Here, the chin was a distinguishing figure of a truly frightening visage.

Consider the terrifying spectacles of vitriol "eating into" the face of Baron Gruner "and dripping from the ears and the chin" in THE ILLUSTRIOUS CLIENT or of "blood dripping down" the chin of Fitzroy McPherson who had "bitten through his lower lip in the paroxysm of his agony" in THE LION'S MANE. Truly, the chin in its normal state is most unremarkable, but unusual circumstances could produce an unusual effect.

For such a usually nondescript feature, the chin enjoyed a varied existence in the Sherlockian stories. Canonical chins could reflect admirable characteristics or add to the virtues of women. They could be handled or hidden or held in unnatural poses. And they could be offensive or even horrible. But, like many other aspects of the Sherlockian saga, they were really never dull.

Doctor Sterndale, the African Explorer

Occasionally, certain people are rightly judged to be "larger than life," so dominant in their personalities and physical attributes that they eclipse all others. These individuals "fill up the room." They command attention and respect. They are remembered long after others are forgotten. Such a man, clearly, was Dr. Leon Sterndale of THE DEVIL'S FOOT. He made a marked impression in the world of Sherlock Holmes, and his personality and the events surrounding his appearance in this story had a significant impact.

Watson's description of the central character in THE DEVIL'S FOOT paints a vivid picture of a larger-than life character:

> Neither of us needed to be told who that visitor was. The huge body, the craggy and deeply seamed face with the fierce eyes and hawk-like nose, the grizzled hair which nearly brushed our cottage ceiling, the beard—golden at the fringes and white near the lips, save for the nicotine stain from his perpetual cigar—all these were as well known in London as in Africa, and could only be associated with the tremendous personality of Dr. Leon Sterndale, the great lion-hunter and explorer.

So, Dr. Sterndale was a celebrity, a man of renown, an African explorer deluxe in the great age of African explorers, a man who might be sought by other adventurers and greeted with an understated, "Dr. Sterndale, I presume?" Holmes and Watson knew of him, and they held Sterndale—a "majestic figure"—in such high esteem that they never "dreamed" of approaching him without an invitation. The very fact that he was such an eminent figure necessarily raises questions about Dr. Sterndale, his background, his work, and his motivations.

Sterndale is described as "a great lion hunter and explorer." He told Holmes that he expected to be "lost for years in Africa." Furthermore, he expanded that thought to say, "I had intended to bury myself in central Africa. My work there is but half finished." But what exactly was Sterndale's "work"? Surely he did more than just wander about hunting lions and looking for the sources of great rivers. Yet, he is described only as being a hunter and explorer, not a medical researcher or humanitarian or businessman or gold miner or diamond seeker or railroad scout or diplomat or slave runner or missionary or double agent or any one of a number of things that he might well have been.

Clues are sparse in THE DEVIL'S FOOT about Dr. Sterndale's mysterious mission in Africa, but they are not totally lacking. Perhaps some indications can be gleaned from the information we have been provided.

Take, for instance, Sterndale's love life. He was consumed with his love for Brenda Tregennis, perhaps even carried on an affair with her, even though he was married. "I have a wife who has left me for years," he told Holmes, and he complained of "the deplorable laws of England" which prevented him from getting a divorce.

Mrs. Sterndale merits a little consideration. Why had she left Dr. Sterndale so many years ago? Was it because of his long absences in Africa? Perhaps his clearly overbearing personality was simply too much for her. Either of these reasons, long absences and a domineering attitude, would have been a huge obstacle for any woman, even Brenda Tregennis. Yet, his young lover seemed unaffected by them. Or was Brenda herself the reason for the separation? That Mrs. Sterndale would not tolerate her husband's affair with "a very beautiful woman" is easily conceivable.

Whatever the reason for his separation from his wife, Dr. Sterndale was in love with Brenda Tregennis—deeply, madly and passionately in love with her. He considered her "an angel upon earth." But the very depth of his feelings for her only deepens the mystery surrounding the nature of his work in Africa. He told Holmes that Brenda was "the only human being whom I have loved or who has ever loved me." They had a relationship marred not only by the shadowy presence of Sterndale's wife, but by their physical separation while he was in Africa. He was willing to "bury" himself in central Africa for years at a time, totally cut off from her. "For years Brenda waited," Sterndale lamented. "For years I waited."

Why, then, would a man so devoted to Brenda Tregennis leave England at all? To hunt lions? To conduct explorations? Bagging lions and finding lost tribes are very interesting activities, but they are optional after all. Yet, having found the love of his life, Sterndale decided to return to Africa. He got as far as Plymouth, but only returned when he learned of Brenda's death.

Since Sterndale was willing to leave Brenda behind, it is reasonable to conclude that his work in Africa was either so important (at least in his own estimation) that he could not forego it or he was under an obligation to someone else (perhaps, even probably, the British government) that he could not escape his duty. He would not make arrangements to take Brenda with him, so it is reasonable to conclude that his work in Africa was dangerous, either because of the usual perils of the unexplored jungle or because he was engaged in a mission that in and of itself was hazardous.

It may be that his work was akin to that of the adventurer Henry Stanley, who spent the years 1879 to 1884 roaming around a vast area of central Africa, cheating native chieftains out of their domains for King Leopold II of Belgium. If so, Sterndale could have been operating on behalf of the British Empire—and under the supervision of Mycroft Holmes, of whom his brother Sherlock observed: "One has to be discreet when one talks of high matters of state. You are right in thinking that he is under the British government. You would also be right in a sense if you said that occasionally he *is* the British government." This was true, not for domestic policy, but for foreign affairs. Mycroft Holmes apparently was involved in all sorts of foreign intrigues and undercover strategies, something of an Ian Fleming-style "M" for the British Secret Service.

Therefore, Sterndale could also have a parallel role in central Africa, appearing to be an explorer, doctor and humanitarian on one hand while operating with a 007-style "license to kill"—a portfolio that permitted his otherwise unacceptable attitude: "I have lived so long among savages and beyond the law . . . that I have got into the way of being a law to myself." He was so confident in that role that he went so far as to threaten even the life of Sherlock Holmes.

Assuming that this is true—that Dr. Sterndale was spending his time in Africa not with the sponsorship of either a missionary or scientific society, but under the direction of the British government itself—other aspects of THE DEVIL'S FOOT take on a different perspective.

Dr. Sterndale had an international reputation, to be sure. He was "as well known in London as in Africa." Yet, he made no attempt to cultivate that reputation. By 1897, he seemed to shun it. Watson writes that Dr. Sterndale's "love of seclusion" was common knowledge. That preference, says Watson, "caused him to spend the greater part of the intervals between his journeys in a small bungalow, buried in the lonely wood of Beauchamp Arriance. Here, amid his books and his maps, he lived an absolutely lonely life, attending to his own simple wants and paying little apparent heed to the affairs of his neighbors."

So Dr. Sterndale spent years at a time traveling around Africa, doing work that was unclear in its nature, and when he returned to England, what did he do? Certainly, not what would be expected. He shut himself off in the woods near a remote village on the Cornish peninsula. There were no visits with his professional colleagues, no lectures on his findings, no interviews with the newspapers. He was every bit as imposing a figure as Professor Challenger, who explored new territories and made new discoveries in *The Lost World*, but unlike Challenger, he had no apparent desire to share that knowledge.

Big egos thrive on recognition, but Dr. Sterndale by this time seemed to avoid not only publicity, but also normal social interaction. He would, in fact, be a perfect candidate for membership in the Diogenes Club, where talking was not allowed, questions were not asked, and people were allowed to be left completely alone.

Interestingly, in Watson's account, the term "buried" is used for his time in England, while the term "bury" is used for his time in Africa. A burial, after all, takes place after a lifetime is concluded. The suggestion seems to be that Dr. Sterndale's reputation was long-established, though not necessarily being supplemented. He was well-known because of his past successes. The British government, perhaps through Mycroft Holmes, enlisted him because of that reputation and because of his ability to travel throughout Africa as a lion-hunter and explorer. He had the perfect cover.

Which leads to a question about the selection of the "placid and sheltered" Poldhu Bay for the convalescence of Sherlock Holmes. A mysterious character by the name of Dr. Moore Agar insisted that Holmes take an extended rest. Holmes made a show of resisting that suggestion, but finally relented. The site selected for Holmes' vacation was the extremely secluded and isolated "Poldhu Bay, at the further extremity of the Cornish peninsula." Watson masterfully described a place that was cut off from the rest of civilization by distance as well as time. Significantly, Sherlock Holmes enjoyed this atmosphere, and Watson wrote: "The glamour and mystery of the place, with its sinister atmosphere of forgotten nations, appealed to imagination of my friend, and he spent much of his time in long walks and solitary meditations upon the moor."

Now, Watson was easily manipulated. He was a steadfast but credulous friend to Sherlock Holmes, and his concern for the great detective's health would make him an unsuspecting foil for a scheme to bring the famous Sherlock Holmes into the same out-of-the-way neighborhood as the equally famous Dr. Leon Sterndale.

Mr. Roundhay, the vicar, claimed to be amateur archaeologist, and "as such Holmes had made his acquaintance." But that may very well have been a ruse as well, a convenient excuse to bring Holmes into contact with Roundhay. The two of them may well have been acting as middle men, through whom Sterndale communicated with the British foreign service.

Of course, Dr. Sterndale could have gone directly to London, met Mycroft Holmes at the Diogenes Club, and passed the information along in that way. Instead he insisted on spending his time in Cornwall. We know, of course, that he had personal business there. He later admitted to Sherlock Holmes that the presence of Brenda Tregennis was "the secret of that Cornish seclusion which people have marveled at."

Those in power in London would be more than willing to indulge what might seem to them to be the eccentric or even paranoid whims of one of their top agents in Africa. If he wanted to retire to Cornwall and exchange his information there, why should they object? If Sterndale was temperamental or demanding about meeting in Cornwall rather than in London—well, arrangements could be made.

Mycroft Holmes himself would not go to Cornwall; that was out of the question. His more active, but equally dependable and discreet brother Sherlock would serve just as well, perhaps even better under the circumstances. The possibility that Mycroft Holmes, Sherlock Holmes, Mr. Roundhay and Dr. Sterndale—even Dr. Moore Agar—were part of an undercover operation of international intrigue involving the race for empire in Africa is not at all farfetched.

Watson did not participate in those "long walks and solitary meditations" that Sherlock Holmes conducted on the moor, nor in the scholarly sessions with Mr. Roundhay. Ample opportunity existed for the exchange of all sorts of information and documents: maps, secret agreements, how much bribe money was needed for a local chieftain, the names and home bases of friendly agents, routes favorable for trade, the location of diamond mines or ivory herds, the discovery of river crossings or mountain passes, the activities of rival powers. In fact, rival powers and individuals acting against the best interests of Britain may well have been a problem especially suited for the formidable Dr. Sterndale.

Perhaps, at some point during his safari explorations, he crossed paths with another famous big-game hunter who, like Sterndale, had a separate and more sinister agenda. That big-game hunter, of course, was Col. Sebastian Moran, who was most famous for his exploits hunting tigers in Asia, but whose book *Three Months in the Jungle* could have been set just as easily in Africa. The similarities between Dr. Sterndale and Col. Moran are remarkable.

His role as a doctor, like that of big-game hunter, would have been of benefit in ways other than just as a cover for his clandestine activities. But exactly what kind of a doctor was Sterndale? We know that his travels took him to West Africa, into the Ubangi country. Of all the plants, herbs, discoveries and relics he might have brought back to England, we know of only one specifically. The devil's-foot root was "shaped like a foot, half human, half goat-like; hence the fanciful name given by a botanical missionary."

Dr. Sterndale revealed its frightful use, as what he called "an ordeal poison." Under the direction of the African witch doctor, "it stimulates the brain centers which control the emotion of fear, and . . . either madness or death is the fate of the unhappy native who is subjected to the ordeal by the priest of his tribe." Why did Sterndale bring back such a dangerous substance? What did he plan to do with it? Well, as a foreign agent, surely he recognized the possibilities for this drug in the cloak-and-dagger world in which he was operating.

In any event, the explorer's relationship with Brenda Tregennis was not connected to his mission in Africa, and neither he nor Mr. Roundhay were likely to have mentioned it to Holmes. Certainly, the death of Sterndale's lover was totally unexpected. Dr. Sterndale was recalled to Cornwall by his confidant Mr. Roundhay, and he want straight to Sherlock Holmes and demanded to know what the detective had learned of the tragedy. His excuse for asking was "unconvincing and inadequate" as far as Sherlock Holmes was concerned. The death of Brenda Tregennis, the insanity of her two brothers, and the subsequent demise of her third brother Mortimer, presented a mystery to Sherlock Holmes quite distinct from the business of foreign intrigue and empire expansion.

Sherlock Holmes solved the case, of course. His investigation revealed that Mortimer Tregennis had killed his own sister and ruined his two brothers for the sake of money. Leon Sterndale had avenged the death of Brenda Tregennis by acting as judge, jury and executioner. In the end, Sherlock Holmes declined to reveal his findings to the police. To the gullible Watson, this was nothing more than another case in which justice was best served by allowing the perpetrator to go free. Holmes had done this before. "I suppose I am committing a felony," he commented in THE BLUE CARBUNCLE, "but it is just possible I am saving a soul."

Now, Dr. Sterndale's soul was almost certainly not the primary consideration for Sherlock Holmes, if it was a consideration at all. He had other matters to think about in Cornwall as he investigated the "Devil's

Foot" mystery. Sterndale's work in Africa in his own estimation was only half finished. "Go and do the other half," said Holmes. "I, at least, am not prepared to prevent you." Not only was Holmes not prepared to prevent Dr. Sterndale's departure, he was probably not really empowered to do so. He knew full well that, even if he turned Sterndale over to the authorities, the British government would quash the case.

They could not afford a man who was so valuable an agent, not to mention being so famous in his own right, to appear in the dock. If Dr. Sterndale had a license to kill in Africa, the extension of that license to Cornwall and its use on such a miserable specimen as Mortimer Tregennis, a man who richly deserved to die and would have hung in any event, was not a matter of concern.

To be sure, the trial of Dr. Sterndale would be an international sensation. Too much might be revealed, too many questions might be asked, too much of British self-interest might be compromised. "I think you must agree, Watson, that it is not a case in which we are called upon to interfere," Holmes insisted. Watson did, indeed, agree, but thought it was a matter of mercy or true justice, rather than a matter of national security. He told his story accordingly, and the true nature of Dr. Sterndale, the African explorer, was never revealed.

A Tale from the Crypt

Unearthing Dracula in Sherlock Holmes

Ask most people who have any kind of understanding of the Canon to recommend a Sherlock Holmes story about vampires, and odds are good that the answer will be THE SUSSEX VAMPIRE. After all, there is a mention of vampires in the title, the client suspects that vampirism is involved, and Holmes even finds two passages in one of his index volumes about vampires. But, when all is said and done, he rejects the whole idea as nothing but rubbish. "What have we to do with walking corpses who can only be held in their grave by stakes driven through their hearts?" he asks Watson. "The world is big enough for us. No ghosts need apply."

Holmes is right, too. He reveals that there is no vampire in Sussex. The blood-sucking in this story is really just benevolent first aid and only subject to what might be understated as "a misunderstanding." If there is a horror story at all in THE SUSSEX VAMPIRE, it could well be *The Omen* or *Children of the Damned* or *The Bad Seed*—any of which might well be based on the horrible little Jacky Ferguson.

There have been other attempts to find vampirism in the Sherlockian canon. In most cases, they turn—not to the undead vampire of Medieval lore who sleeps in a coffin filled with his native earth by day while drinking the blood of the living by night—but instead to what might be considered "psychic vampires."

Barbara Roden, in the 1993 edition of *The Journal of The Arthur Conan Doyle Society*, gave us a wonderful definition of a "psychic vampire":

> These are creatures who do not resort to such crudities as sucking blood or turning into bats. They do not shun the daylight or sleep in coffins; instead, they appropriate the life forces of their victims by draining them of energy, willpower, and, in some cases, the will to live.

The best example of a "psychic vampire" in the stories of Arthur Conan Doyle is his short story JOHN BARRINGTON COWLES, which was published in 1884. In it, Kate Northcott has a mysterious and evil influence over her prospective husbands. One of them is John Barrington Cowles, who cries out in anguish:

> Oh, Kate, Kate! . . . I pictured you an angel and I find you . . . a fiend! A vampire soul behind a lovely face.

Conan Doyle also uses this same theme, a woman's malevolent, psychological sapping of the will, in his 1894 story THE PARASITE.

As far as the Sherlockian canon is concerned, there are two cases involving this so-called "psychic vampirism." One is THE CARDBOARD BOX, in which Sarah Cushing uses her power and evil influence over her sister Mary and Mary's husband Jim. The other is THE THREE GABLES, in which Isadora Klein—twice referred to as a fiend—saps Douglas Maberley of his energy and willpower. In both cases, death results from the terrible activities of the "psychic vampire."

Interestingly, in all of these Conan Doyle stories—THE SUSSEX VAMPIRE, JOHN BARRINGTON COWLES, THE PARASITE, THE CARDBOARD BOX and THE THREE GABLES—and in another, UNCLE JEREMY'S HOUSEHOLD—the vampire-like character is a woman, not at all the masculine, male vampire we know from folklore; not at all the predator who exudes not only a supernatural force from the undead, but also a barely disguised sexual attraction.

These vampires or suspected vampires are not really what we usually associate with the term, and as a result, they are unsatisfying as vampire-like figures. Psychic vampires are really no fun—too much Sigmund Freud and too little Wes Craven. What we want is the real thing, a classic vampire—a cape-wearing, woman-stalking, mesmerizing, evil-eyed, threatening, dangerous, powerful, plotting vampire. We want the kind of vampire who merits an old-fashioned showdown, a duel to the death, a character so bad-to-the-bone that he has to be destroyed, for the benefit of all that is decent and noble and good.

Fortunately, we have such a character in the Sherlock Holmes stories. Oh, he is no ghost, either. He doesn't really drink the blood of the living, at least not in a literal way. Sherlock Holmes, as always, is right about that sort of thing. It's rubbish. Even so, there should be no misunderstanding about vampires in the Canon. There is indeed a vampire figure, and there is indeed a story that parallels in far too many ways to be coincidental, the most famous and influential vampire tale of all time. In fact, we have a retelling of that tale. So consider, if you will, this familiar story line:

- A murderous aristocrat from Central Europe, with a history of violence and death behind him, moves to England in search of fresh victims.
- He leases a large house, which serves as his base of operations. He has unusual power and influence over women—a power he uses for evil.
- While in England, he destroys one woman and sets his sights on another—a woman of exceptional qualities.
- His threat to this woman is recognized by her friends and protectors, who are determined to save her.
- They call on the most knowledgeable and accomplished expert they can find to help; and he is assisted in his efforts by his trusted friend, a medical doctor.
- Despite being a brilliant and totally ruthless foe who has anticipated almost every obstacle in his path, the villain is defeated and his intended victim is rescued.

This, of course, is the plot of *Dracula*, Bram Stoker's most famous novel, which was published in 1897. The book has never been out of print, and it has been read and re-read by millions. The story has been told and retold on film many times as well, and perhaps that is where most of us have learned about Dracula. The details have entered popular culture as surely as have the details of Tom Sawyer and Huckleberry Finn, of Dorothy and her trip to Oz, of Superman and the circumstances which brought him to earth. So we recognize this story line as the story of Dracula. Much of the book is concerned with the efforts of Professor Abraham van Helsing to protect the lovely Mina Harker from the designs of the vampire Count Dracula.

But as Sherlockians, we should also recognize this same story line, in every single detail, as that of one of Sherlock Holmes' sixty recorded adventures. Because this exact same story line, in every single detail, is that of THE ILLUSTRIOUS CLIENT, in which Sherlock Holmes is retained to protect the lovely Violet de Merville from the designs of the murderous Baron Adelbert Gruner.

THE ILLUSTRIOUS CLIENT appeared in print for the first time in 1924. That Arthur Conan Doyle (or Dr. John H. Watson) was familiar with such a successful and popular novel as *Dracula* cannot be doubted, but finding an admission from either of those worthy men of letters that the plot was actually "lifted" is almost certainly not going to happen. Instead, we must consider the evidence. Using "the story line" as described, there are 18 major points of similarity between these two famous tales—more than enough to dispel any idea that all of these similarities are simply coincidence.

A murderous aristocrat from Central Europe,

Both Baron Adelbert Gruner of Austria, the villain of THE ILLUSTRIOUS CLIENT and Count Dracula of Transylvania were members of one of the numerous aristocratic families of Europe. These two characters were among many who claimed titles which often reached far back into history.

Dracula is popularly identified with Vlad III, a very real ruler of Walachia who was actually born in Transylvania and who lived in the 15th Century, from 1431 to 1476. Both Walachia and Transylvania are part of modern-day Romania. In real life, Vlad III was a prince, although in Stoker's novel he is given the title of Count. He is considered an important figure in Romanian history because he managed to unify Walachia and resisted the influences of foreign powers, including, and perhaps especially, the Turks.

As for Gruner, there might be some justification to question the validity of his title of "Baron." Often, such titles were of doubtful origin, and imposters and pretenders were common; and London was a magnet for such characters. England was insulated in many ways from the rest of Europe, and con men using an aristocratic title would find easy pickings in the society hostesses of the Victorian Era. A charming "Baron" from a remote part of Europe would add quite a bit of interest to a dinner party in London or a hunting weekend in the country.

However, in this case, it appears that Gruner really was a "Baron." Sherlock Holmes already knew about Gruner and about his crimes, and it seems unlikely that Holmes would not also know or suspect him of being an imposter if his credentials were not in order. After all, Holmes pointed out to Sir James Damery that he considered it his "business to follow the details of Continental crime."

Gruner clearly was a man of considerable influence, since he was able to escape a murder charge on a technicality; and of considerable wealth, since he pursued an extravagantly expensive hobby as a collector of Chinese porcelain; and of considerable standing, since he was allowed to be a part of a "select" company participating in that Mediterranean yachting voyage, where he met Violet de Merville. Like Dracula, Gruner was an authentic member of the European aristocracy. And like Dracula, he was a particularly evil one.

with a history of violence and death behind him,

Sherlock Holmes knew all about Baron Gruner, and identified him immediately as "the Austrian murderer." Holmes had no doubt of his guilt in the death of his wife and of a potential witness. Murder was an essential part of his portfolio. He was ruthless and arrogant, living apparently without the benefit of a conscience, destroying those who stood in his way, and both mocking and threatening those who dared to challenge him.

Gruner was as dangerous and malignant as any opponent who ever faced Sherlock Holmes, including Professor Moriarty. And surely Gruner was not contemporary in London with Charles Augustus Milverton, because Baron Gruner was clearly an even worse specimen of humanity. Had those two competed head-to-head for the title of "worst man in London," there is every reason to believe that Gruner would have won hands down.

Meanwhile, we are told in Chapter 23 of Bram Stoker's account that Count Dracula had left a trail of death over a period of "centuries" in Europe. Professor Van Helsing states in Chapter 18 that: "The vampire . . . cannot die by mere passing of the time, he can flourish when he can fatten on the blood of the living."

While Vlad III was an important military and political figure in the history of Romania, he is remembered around the world today for his cruelty. He is known, not as Vlad III, but as Vlad Tepes, or "Vlad the Impaler." He earned this title because his favorite form of execution was impalement—hoisting the victims onto huge, sharpened stakes and leaving them to die. This was a slow, excruciatingly painful manner of death, and Vlad apparently took an intense sadistic pleasure in seeing it administered. He would even set up a banquet table and dine as he watched people die.

Vlad's own subjects gave him another nickname: Dracul, meaning "dragon" or "devil," and thus Dracula. Vlad, then, was the son of the devil. The tales of his gruesome executions, of individuals and of large groups, are truly horrible. He reportedly impaled 20,000 Turkish prisoners at one time. Otherwise, he may have killed from 40,000 to 100,000 of his own subjects.

There is no question that a "history of violence and death" belonged to both Baron Gruner and to Count Dracula, both as he is described in the novel and as he is described in history.

moves to England in search of fresh victims.

Baron Gruner "had come to England," established himself, and attached himself pretty quickly to Violet de Merville, to whom he was engaged. This was no surprise to Sherlock Holmes, who knew about the Baron's presence in England. Holmes said that he "had a presentiment that sooner or later he would find me some work to do." Perhaps Europe had become uncomfortable for the Baron. While he may have beaten the rap on the killing of his wife, his reputation was not so easily repaired. A cool reception in continental society; the prospect, perhaps, of revenge from his former in-laws; or simply an excellent opportunity for gain and for the pursuit of his sadistic pleasures. These were the reasons that Baron Gruner set up his operations in England.

Count Dracula seems to have had an even bigger agenda: "He came to London to invade a new land," we are told in Chapter 25. Of course we know that London was the greatest city in the world at that time. Dr. Watson tells us in the very first chapter of *A Study in Scarlet* that London was a "great cesspool into which all the loungers and idlers of the Empire are irresistibly drained." A great, vibrant city, full of people of all sorts, full not only of people of substance and standing, but also of hundreds of thousands of the lower classes, people who could—and often did—disappear without a trace, without anyone to ask more than a question or two about them, if even that.

How Dracula must have enjoyed the idea of this kind of city, pulsating with human life, filled with potential victims of his blood thirst. What a contrast that must have been to the thinly populated, stagnant, depressed and poverty-stricken land of Transylvania. Dracula had taken all he could from his native land. Jonathan Harker was brought to Castle Dracula, remember, not to be a victim of Dracula and his brides, but to be a facilitator of the Count's move from one of the most remote parts of Europe to one of the most bustling cities the world had ever known.

Both Baron Gruner and Count Dracula recognized London as a place of opportunity and as a fresh source of easy prey.

He leases a large house, which serves as his base of operations.

Of course, an appropriate setting and an effective base of operations in London was necessary for both of these two villains. This was a practical consideration that was not neglected by either of them.

Baron Gruner set up his household at Vernon Lodge, near Kingston, in what was described as "a large house." His house met his needs socially and was suitable for his extensive collection.

We learn in Chapter 8 that Dracula's house in England was at Carfax, near Purfleet, and was used primarily as a place to "sleep" during the sunlit hours. The house had been standing empty before being rented by Dracula, and 50 boxes of earth were delivered to a "partially ruined building" which formed a part of the house and grounds. Like Gruner, Dracula had found a house which suited his needs very well.

He has unusual power and influence over women—
Baron Gruner was a ladies man, one of those guys with a magnetic attraction to women. Sir James Damery recognized this element of the dilemma when he visited Sherlock Holmes and Dr. Watson:

> The fellow is, as you may have heard, extraordinarily handsome, with a most fascinating manner, a gentle voice, and that air of romance and mystery which means so much to a woman. He is said to have the whole sex at his mercy and to have made ample use of the fact.

This is a major frustration for Violet de Merville's would-be protectors. They know what a bad actor he is, but his power and influence over her is almost unbreakable. Again, Sir James Damery:

> The villain attached himself to the lady, and with such effect that he has completely and absolutely won her heart. To say that she loves him hardly expresses it. She dotes upon him; she is obsessed by him. Outside of him there is nothing on earth. She will not hear one word against him. Everything has been done to cure her of her madness, but in vain. To sum up, she proposes to marry him next month. As she is of age and has a will of iron, it is hard to know how to prevent her.

Just as Gruner had an almost supernatural ability to control Violet de Merville and, presumably, the many other women he seduced, used, and tossed aside, Dracula possessed a power over women that was every bit as great, if not greater.

Interestingly, both of these villains boasted about their ability to manipulate and control women. "I have been fortunate enough to win the entire affection of this lady," Baron Gruner told Sherlock Holmes. And Count Dracula declared to Dr. Seward and the others allied against him in Chapter 23 that "Your girls that you all love are mine already." Mina

Harker states in Chapter 19 of *Dracula*: "I was powerless to act, my feet and my hands and my brain were weighted." She confesses in Chapter 21 that "I did not want to hinder him." Once Count Dracula had bitten one of his victims, she was not only powerless to resist, she was unwilling to resist—just like Violet de Merville.

a power he uses for evil.

Neither Baron Gruner nor Count Dracula had any element in their motivations or actions that was not pure evil. Gruner's approach to women was malignant and sadistic. Kitty Winter described it this way:

> I tell you, Mr. Homes, this man collects women, and takes a pride in his collection, as some men collect moths or butterflies. He had it all in that book. Snapshot photographs, names, details, everything about them. It was a beastly book—a book no man, even if he had come from the gutter, could have put together. But it was Adelbert Gruner's book all the same. 'Souls I have ruined.' He could have put that on the outside if he had been so minded.

The appeal of the vampire to women, the subtext of sexual appeal and sexual tension, is a constant theme not only in *Dracula*, but in virtually every manifestation of vampire mythology, literature and popular culture.

Stoker certainly had to be aware of the latent sexual themes of his novel. Seduction by Count Dracula turned women into lustful sirens and horrible baby-killers—just the opposite of the Victorian ideal of chaste and nurturing womanhood. Penetration by the fangs of the vampire is both violent and erotic, but leads to the destruction of the woman concerned. Likewise, illicit sex in Victorian times raised the prospect of at least social stigma, if not pregnancy or disease, leading just as surely to the destruction of the woman concerned.

How many times have we wondered why good girls have such an attraction to bad boys? Baron Gruner and Count Dracula are fascinating, have no concept of their own mortality and are shamelessly lustful. They don't obey the rules. They live on the edge of society. They don't even bother to hide their true natures—remember that Gruner told Violet de Merville "every unsavory public scandal of his past life," and it made no difference to her. If Gruner and Dracula are recognized as dangerous, they are also deemed to be exciting.

While in England, he destroys one woman

Baron Gruner's first English victim was Kitty Winter, who felt compelled to try to warn Violet of the danger she was facing from Baron Gruner:

> I am his last mistress. I am one of a hundred that he has tempted and used and ruined and thrown into the refuse heap, as he will you also. Your refuse heap is more likely to be a grave, and maybe that's the best.
>
> I tell you, you foolish woman, if you marry this man he'll be the death of you. It may be a broken heart or it may be a broken neck, but he'll have you one way or the other.

Chillingly, Kitty Winter tells Holmes that "what I am Adelbert Gruner made me." This is a statement full of meaning, and it has a direct parallel in *Dracula*. Lucy Westenra, Count Dracula's first English victim, finally succumbed to the bite of the vampire, and after her untimely death, she became what van Helsing in Chapter 15 called "Un-Dead." Just as Kitty Winter was what Gruner made her, so was Lucy what Dracula had made her.

The bitterness of Kitty Winter's feeling toward Baron Gruner would lead us to believe that her life was utterly ruined, and only death would release her. Lucy Westenra rested in her grave only after being destroyed by Professor van Helsing and his colleagues (Chapter 16).

and sets his sights on another—

The ultimate fate of both Violet de Merville and Mina Harker might have been their ultimate destruction—death was intended for both of them.

Violet de Merville was to be the bride of Baron Gruner, once he had finished with Kitty Winter and destroyed her life. Sherlock Holmes recognized her as a future victim, calling her—in another phrase that calls Dracula to mind—"a woman who has to submit to be caressed by bloody hands and lecherous lips."

Baron Gruner's aims were selfish and evil. He had "expensive tastes," collecting books, art and Chinese pottery. So he undoubtedly was after whatever family fortune that Violet de Merville might possess. But he had more in mind for her. We know of his sadistic nature, so the kind of life she would have had with him can only be imagined—although that life probably would not have lasted for long. Domination, embezzlement, and ultimately murder when she was no longer needed was her certain fate.

Once Lucy Westenra was out of the way, Count Dracula declared in Chapter 21 that he intended to make Mina Harker "my companion and helper." Dracula's designs on Mina Harker were just as nefarious as Gruner's plans for Violet de Merville. Dracula had a lustful desire for Mina, of course. He wanted to make her his undead partner, his vampire bride, sharing his nightly hunt for the fresh blood of human victims, and joining him in his reign of fear and death. Through Mina and his other vampire brides, Dracula declared to Professor van Helsing and his companions, "you and others shall yet be mine, my creatures, to do my bidding and to be my jackals when I want to feed." So Dracula viewed Mina not only as a beautiful victim and a desirable mate, but also as a tool to thwart the opposition of van Helsing and his allies.

a woman of exceptional qualities.
Violet de Merville was described by Sir James Damery as "young, rich, beautiful, accomplished, a wonder-woman in every way." Sherlock Holmes himself was not immune to recognizing the exceptional qualities of Violet de Merville, while lamenting the influence that the evil Baron Gruner had over her:

> She is beautiful, but with the ethereal other-world beauty of some fanatic whose thoughts are set on high. I have seen such faces in the pictures of the old masters of the Middle Ages. How a beastman could have laid his vile paws upon such a being of the beyond I cannot imagine. You may have noticed how extremes call to each other, the spiritual to the animal, the cave-man to the angel. You never saw a worse case than this.

This idea of a spiritual superiority of the woman is also found in *Dracula*. The Count's intended victim, Mina Harker, was described in Chapter 14 as "one of God's women, fashioned by his own hand to show us men and other women that there is a heaven ... So true, so sweet, so noble, so little an egoist ..."

His threat to this woman is recognized by her friends and protectors,
Gruner may have been able to fool Violet de Merville and a parade of other women before her, but his true nature was well understood by a cadre of men who had their own base of power and influence. Allied in the effort to save Violet de Merville were Sir James Damery, who brought the case the Sherlock Holmes; General de Merville, her father; and the unnamed "Illustrious Client" who took a "paternal interest" in her. Joining

this cause, of course, were Holmes, Dr. Watson, and Shinwell Johnson. Their mission, according to Sir James, was simply put: "It is this . . . lovely, innocent girl, whom we are endeavoring to save from the clutches of a fiend."

The group which banded together to save Mina Harker from the clutches of another fiend, Count Dracula, were Arthur Holmwood (Lord Godalming); Jonathan Harker, her husband; and the colorful American, Quincy P. Morris. Joining in this cause were Professor van Helsing and Dr. Seward. Like Violet, Mina had benevolent friends, and van Helsing noted in Chapter 27 that "Some men so loved her that they did dare much for her sake."

who are determined to save her.

The lives of worthy women were at stake in both THE ILLUSTRIOUS CLIENT and *Dracula*. "To revenge crime is important, but to prevent it is more so," says Sir James as he solicits the help of Sherlock Holmes, who more often was called upon to solve crimes rather than prevent them.

Professor van Helsing agreed with such an approach, stating in Chapter 16: "But there remains a greater task, to find out the author of all this sorrow and to stamp him out."

The saving of these women was not without risk. Quincy Morris gave his life in the effort to protect Mina Harker. Sherlock Holmes suffered a severe beating, the worst injuries of his life, putting him on the verge of death, in the effort to protect Violet de Merville.

They call on the most knowledgeable and accomplished expert they can find to help;

Violet de Merville's protectors turned to Sherlock Holmes, a man of "great powers" and a "well-deserved reputation." No one needs to be reminded of the abilities of Sherlock Holmes. He had an encyclopedic knowledge of criminals, an international reputation for dealing with difficult problems, a willingness to pursue solutions outside of the usual and predictable methods of others, and confidence in the knowledge that his unique insights are correct.

In Chapter 9 of *Dracula,* we learn that the expert assistance needed for the situation was sought from "Professor van Helsing of Amsterdam, who knows as much about obscure diseases as any one in the world . . . He is a seemingly arbitrary man; this is because he knows what he is talking about better than anyone else."

All those attributes listed for Sherlock Holmes have their counterparts in Professor van Helsing as well: an encyclopedic knowledge of vampires, an international reputation, a willingness to act outside of the usual bounds of law or medicine, and confidence in the knowledge that his unique insights are correct. If the entire Sherlockian canon is taken into account, the parallels between Holmes and van Helsing would be too numerous to mention here. Overall, the methods utilized by both Holmes and van Helsing might be unorthodox, but they are based on a logical, disciplined and orderly approach to the problem at hand.

and he is assisted in his efforts by his trusted friend, a medical doctor.
The doctor in THE ILLUSTRIOUS CLIENT is none other than Dr. John H. Watson, M.D., late of the Army Medical Department, a graduate of the University of London, who was friend, associate, housemate, confidant and chronicler of Sherlock Holmes, who—in this case—helped Holmes break into the home of Baron Gruner.

In *Dracula*, Dr. John Seward, M.D., was a friend, pupil, and confidant of Professor van Helsing, who—in this case—helped van Helsing break into the home of the vampire Count.

Further connections and parallels should be noted: both were named John, both—unlike their mentors—are known to enjoy happy marriages during their lifetimes, and both had provided medical attention to their expert friends. Of course, Watson helped tend to Sherlock Holmes as he recovered from the beating Baron Gruner's agents had administered to him. And, in an eerie foreshadowing of the later events of the novel, van Helsing mentions in one of his letters that Dr. Seward had once sucked gangrene from a wound that van Helsing had suffered (Chapter 9).

Despite facing a brilliant
Baron Gruner is described as "a brilliant, forceful rascal" as well as "cunning" and as a man with "a complex mind." Likewise, van Helsing described Dracula as "the cleverest and most cunning" of foes in Chapter 18. And in Chapter 23, van Helsing testifies that Dracula had a "mighty brain, a learning beyond compare."

Note that both accounts specifically attribute three qualities to both Dracula and Gruner: intellectual brilliance; enlightenment—that is, the ability to put that intellectual ability to practical use; and cunning. These were no ordinary adversaries. No ordinary heroes were needed to defeat them, and the victory of good over evil was not a foregone conclusion.

Both of these tales are adventures, of course, and they ultimately require physical action and courageous activity. Holmes comes face to face with Gruner, just as van Helsing comes face to face with Dracula. But the battle between the heroes and their foes is a battle of wills and of intellect.

and totally ruthless foe

Sir James Damery had no illusions about Baron Gruner's murderous tendencies: "I should say there is no more dangerous man in Europe" than Baron Gruner, he said, a man "with whom violence is familiar and who will, literally, stick at nothing."

Van Helsing likewise held no illusions about Count Dracula, who he says in Chapter 23 possessed "a heart that knew no fear and no remorse." Van Helsing noted in Chapter 18 that Dracula could be described as both heartless and "callous."

It goes without saying that Gruner and Dracula were without conscience and unwilling to let anyone or anything stop them. A description of their facial expressions, perhaps, demonstrates their ruthlessness as well as anything:

Of Gruner, Watson says the following:

> His hair and moustache were raven black, the latter short, pointed, and carefully waxed. His features were regular and pleasing, save only his straight, thin-lipped mouth. If ever I saw a murderer's mouth it was there—a cruel, hard gash in the face, compressed, inexorable, and terrible.

We know that Dracula wore a long, white moustache, and Dr. Seward's diary (Chapter 23) has this account of the appearance of the vampire:

> As the Count saw us, a horrible sort of snarl passed over his face, showing the eyeteeth long and pointed. But the evil smile as quickly passed into a cold stare of lion-like disdain. His expression again changed as, with a single impulse, we all advanced upon him . . . The expression of the Count's face was . . . hellish.

who has anticipated almost every obstacle in his path,

Baron Gruner anticipated his opposition and prepared for it. "The cunning devil has told her every unsavory public scandal of his past life, but always in such a way as to make himself out to be an innocent martyr. She absolutely accepts his version and will listen to no other." Such an approach worked to disarm his detractors.

Van Helsing was frustrated by Count Dracula's strategic moves as well: "Everything has been carefully thought out, and done systematically and with precision," he says in Chapter 17. "He seemed to have been prepared for every obstacle which might be placed . . . in the way of his intentions being carried out."

the villain is defeated

Not only were the plots and schemes of both Baron Gruner and Count Dracula thwarted, they were both destroyed physically. Kitty Winter's vitriol attack on the man who had victimized her—an attack that took place in his own home—was devastating:

> The Baron uttered a horrible cry . . . He clapped his two hands to his face and rushed round the room . . . while scream after scream resounded through the house . . . The features were blurred, discolored, inhuman, terrible.

For Count Dracula, the end—at the very threshold of his castle—was also gruesome, as described in Chapter 27:

> He "was deathly pale, just like a waxen image . . . But, on the instant came the sweep and flash of Jonathan's great knife. I shrieked as I saw it shear through the throat . . . It was like a miracle, but before our very eyes, and almost in the drawing of a breath, the whole body crumbled into dust and passed from our sight.

Extraordinary means were required to put these villains out of action. For both Gruner and Dracula, a grotesque physical disfigurement or dismemberment was needed to render them powerless to victimize others in the future.

and his intended victim is rescued.

"The effect at any rate, was all that could be desired . . . the marriage between Baron Adelbert Gruner and Miss Violet de Merville would not take place," we are told at the conclusion of THE ILLUSTRIOUS CLIENT. And, presumably, because of his disfigurement, Gruner's career of victimizing and murdering women was ended as well.

Van Helsing, succinctly for a change, as he is one of the most verbose characters in all of fiction, described the ultimate effect of the demise of the vampire in Chapter 27 thusly: "Now God be thanked that all has not been in vain . . . The curse has passed away!"

Conclusion

Under the law, a fingerprint is matched beyond doubt with as few as seven points of similarity. In some countries, as many as 16 are required. Yet, 18 major points have been presented to detail the parallels between

THE ILLUSTRIOUS CLIENT and *Dracula*. Far more could be considered—the attentive reader could find dozens of smaller similarities in plot, in theme and in characters.

In fact, the major characters themselves provide mirror images:

- Sherlock Holmes and van Helsing, the experts and the heroes.
- Dr. Watson and Dr. Seward, their faithful assistants.
- Baron Gruner and Count Dracula, the evil and murderous adversaries.
- Kitty Winter and Lucy Westenra, the innocent first victims, destroyed by the villains.
- Violet de Merville and Mina Harker, the outstanding women in need of deliverance, the focus of mighty efforts to save them and defeat the evil-doers.

Even some of the minor characters may have parallels, though they are less pronounced. For instance, the American cowboy Quincy Morris of *Dracula* describes himself as a "rough fellow," and he calls to mind "Porky" Shinwell Johnson of THE ILLUSTRIOUS CLIENT. Arthur Holmwood, Lord Godalming, the fiancé of Lucy Westenra, might find a fainter counterpart in Sir James Damery, also of the aristocracy. And Jonathan Harker, nearly put out of commission altogether by Dracula has a kindred spirit in General de Merville, who was on the verge of being completely broken by Baron Gruner.

So, there we have it. The evidence is strong. The connection surely can no longer be denied. All that remains is an explanation: Why are these two stories so strikingly similar? Why are their plots essentially the same? Was it coincidence? Piracy? A subtle tribute by Conan Doyle or Dr. Watson to the classic tale written by Bram Stoker?

Or, perhaps, could it have been something more than this—something truly disturbing and sinister, something from the realm of the unknown?

I leave it to the reader to form your own conclusions, as we pursue our own adventures in the world of Sherlock Holmes.

A Musical Toast to Nathan Garrideb

G-A-doubleR-I-D-E-B spells Garrideb.
He's a man who had a real unique name.
Sherlock Holmes ensured that he would know fame.
He had hopes that he'd be
Rich beyond his dreams.
But he was bound to be let down
And he eventually found
That he was just as poor as me.

Now, Nathan was a recluse
Who only had much real use
For cabinets full of odd and funny stuff:
A bunch of fossil bones,
Or coins from lands unknown,
Or butterflies or moths or aged flints.

His only interest was
To fill that ancient vase
With even more of his collection's needs.
But he had no thought that he
Was right on top of the
Machinery to make his dreams come true.

So what can we all learn
From this man who took his turn
Among Sherlock's list of clients needing aid?
Well, first we should all see
That collecting things can be
A path to madness, poverty or worse.

Sherlockians are known
To keep pursuing tomes
Or monographs now listed in DeWaal.
But we should all accept
That there's always much that's left,
And we'll never, ever live to get it all.

The Hans Sloan of his age,
Garrideb must take a page
From Scrooge or other single-minded men.
The world keeps moving on.
1895 is gone.
So these interludes are great, but they must end.

A visit to the past
Should be times to last
An evening or a day, but not your life.
Nathan gives us pleasure
When we read of him in leisure,
And Sherlock once again declines to fail.

So we should keep in mind,
Garrideb, one of a kind,
Gave his name to one more Holmes and Watson tale.
Thus, he will live for ages
In Watson's timeless pages,
As real as any hero, knave or king.

G-A-doubleR-I-D-E-B spells Garrideb.
He's a man who had a real unique name.
Sherlock Holmes ensured that he would know fame.
We will never forget
His comic-tragic tale.
So lift your glass, or a flask,
Or stick your head into a cask,
And drink to Garrideb, Nathan Garrideb, to you.

Between the Lines

Thoughts on Sherlock Holmes and Two Remarkable Women

A great service would be performed if there could be, once and for all, an authoritative debunking of the rampant—but totally unfounded—speculation about a "relationship" between Sherlock Holmes and Irene Adler Norton. As everyone knows, she was regarded as *the* woman by the Master Detective because of her success in outwitting him in A SCANDAL IN BOHEMIA. Building on this statement, the world of pastiche is infested with stories about a romance between the two. The more objectionable of them go so far as to produce marriage and/or progeny from the couple.

This is done, apparently, because of a curious reluctance to allow Holmes to pursue his life without the emotional entanglements that are central to most other people. In addition, this is done obstinately and shamelessly despite the plain testimony of Dr. Watson: "It was not that he felt any emotion akin to love for Irene Adler. All emotions, and that one particularly, were abhorrent to his cold, precise, but admirably balanced mind."

Such a statement, in and of itself, ought to be enough to banish the impudent and offensive attempts to link the two, either emotionally or physically, from Holmes-inspired literature once and for all. However, there are three other very good reasons to remove Irene Adler Norton from any scenario that pertains to the private life of Sherlock Holmes.

First, she was a "well-known adventuress." That is, she was a professional mistress "of dubious and questionable memory." Why Holmes would want to bind himself to such a woman—used (in fact, well-used) goods—never has been adequately explained. A man of his standing in the Victorian age, a men descended from the landed gentry, would not lower himself in his own eyes or the eyes of others by cavorting with her.

Second, she was married. She married a lawyer, who presumably was lacking in either scruples (which is not difficult to believe) or good judgment (being blinded by love) and thus would have none of the reluctance of an upright and knowledgeable citizen like Holmes. On the other hand, Mr. Norton may have been totally unaware of her background. In an case, Sherlock Holmes knew she was married. He had, after all, facilitated the ceremony. Whatever we might think of Holmes, surely we do not believe he was a partner in adultery.

Third, she was dead. This is a clincher. Remember, Watson referred to her as "the late Irene Adler" and recalled her "memory." The case took place in March of 1888, and Watson's account was published in 1891. A period of only three years is available for the theorists to have her fall out of love with her husband, get a divorce (no quick process at the time), and return . . . not to the high-rolling world of millionaire playboys, but to the arms of the Spartan-living Sherlock Holmes to share secret liaisons or even babies—all without Watson's knowledge. The newly-married doctor may have been preoccupied and somewhat thick, but not *that* thick. Too little time, too little opportunity, too little likelihood—the starry-eyed romance novelists must look elsewhere for their fodder.

So the hypothesis romantically linking Irene Adler Norton to Sherlock Holmes fails. Unfortunately, the theorists are unwilling to abandon completely this popular and enduring, if distasteful, myth. Therefore, there have been attempts to create new ones, with other female characters from the canon. One such attempt that enjoyed recent vogue substituted the lovely Maud Bellamy for Mrs. Norton based on an expansive description penned many years later by a retired Sherlock Holmes himself in THE LION'S MANE.

A close analysis of Holmes' ruminations on Maud Bellamy, however, appears to disprove any idea that she commanded a romantic interest for the Master Detective or even that she could replace or supplant the late Mrs. Norton in his estimation. Consider, if you will, his actual statements and reasonable bit of "between the lines" dissection of them. Here is what Holmes had to say about Miss Bellamy and what he may well have been thinking:

"There is no gainsaying she would have graced any assembly in the world."
I haven't been studying human nature all this time for nothing. I know full well how a woman like this can be "excellent for drawing the veil from men's motives and actions."

"Who could have imagined that so rare a flower would grow from such a root and in such an atmosphere?"

Part of solving any case is winnowing the ordinary from the exotic. The very fact that she is different from every other woman in this part of the country may have significance.

"Women have seldom been an attraction for me, for my brain has always governed my heart . . ."
And when I say "always," I mean it. I have lived like one of Poe's neurotic narrators, who said, "In the strange anomaly of my existence, feelings with me had never been of the heart, and my passions always were of the mind." Even Irene Adler, the woman, fascinated me only because she alone of her sex was my intellectual peer.

" . . . but I could not look upon her perfect clear-cut face, with all the soft freshness of the Downlands in her delicate coloring . . ."
This specimen bears up well under the kind of observation I advocated in "The Book of Life." How remarkable that there is not the slightest blemish or irregularity in her! However, her home county would be an easy enough deduction for me, wherever I might meet her.

" . . . without realizing that no young man would cross her path unscathed."
Fortunately, I am not a young man—there will be no losing of my senses over a pretty face. I resolved long ago to remain unshaken by purely physical charms; and at this point in my life, I would justly be considered an "old fool" for even looking her way.

"Such was the girl who had pushed open the door and stood now, wide-eyed and intense, in front of Harold Stackhurst."
Yes, she's a girl, not a woman. To me, that's no small difference. However, as I said before, some young man will gladly take her for his own.

These were the first impressions that Maud Bellamy made upon Sherlock Holmes, but her subsequent actions could not help but impress him favorably. She was dealing with the death of her fiancé without any feminine hysterics, and she had asserted her independence of mind in the face of the forceful demands of her father and brother. Holmes had further reflections on this uncommon woman:

"She listened . . . with a composed concentration which showed me that she possessed strong character as well as great beauty."
Thank goodness, we have not endured the weeping and wailing of some vapid damsel in distress. That would be Watson's department, in the old days. But Miss

Bellamy turns out to be an excellent witness and a fine example of how a woman ought to behave.

"Maud Bellamy will always remain in my memory as a most complete and remarkable woman."

I cannot imagine that Miss Bellamy continued to reside in this part of the country, considering all of her charms. London is the place for her. Perhaps it is for the best that she lives for me "in my memory" rather than in my daily experience. Doubtless, I would have been disappointed more than once with the failings common to her sex.

Indeed, Holmes might have felt some twinges of disappointment even before the conclusion of THE LION'S MANE matter. Despite Miss Bellamy's excellent qualities, Holmes described her as looking at him "helplessly" and noted that "she blushed and seemed confused." To Sherlock Holmes, she was only a girl after all. No wonder he felt compelled to be kind, to condescend, to tell her a little white lie: "I value a woman's instinct in such matters." Of course, nothing could be farther from the truth.

Even so, Holmes looked upon her with a degree of approval that few women had been able to earn. Certainly, Maud Bellamy belonged to an elite set of women who commanded the admiration and esteem of Sherlock Holmes—a group that, until that time, may have been no larger than Irene Adler Norton and Mrs. Hudson (although a case can be made for at least a few others).

That Sherlock Holmes had no romantic interest in either Mrs. Norton or Miss Bellamy should not lessen either of them in the eyes of the world. No woman was so honored, but these two merited his respect—and that is no small thing. There is no need to "replace" Irene with Maud or anyone else as Sherlock Holmes' love interest. Let Sherlock be Sherlock, a man who "never spoke of the softer passions, save with a gibe and a sneer."

Dead? Not Hardly!

"I heard you were dead," asserts one bad guy after another to the very much alive and always formidable John Wayne in *Big Jake* (1971). "Not hardly," he'd reply before delivering either a beating or a bullet to the offender. The same statement was directed repeatedly to the estimable, but clearly exasperated, Snake Plissken (Kurt Russell) in *Escape from New York* (1981) just before he turned the futuristic prison society on its ear.

As anyone who has ever watched a television soap opera knows full well, if you don't actually see someone die, convincingly and completely, with face intact, and without an identical twin, and then actually see the body go into the grave, with dirt piled on top and packed down firmly—well, that person more than likely really isn't dead. "I'll be back" is written all over the last scene. Fiery car wrecks, lost planes, falls off cliffs, and reports of a plague in a remote Mexican village are all notoriously unreliable affirmations of death. The soap opera character not only can, but certainly will, reappear—usually after the "surviving" spouse has married a best friend, relative or bitter enemy. Amnesia is a convenient partner in such plots. It occurs approximately twelve thousand percent more often in soap operas than in real life.

Now, don't misunderstand. We're not talking about the "living dead" *a la* Dracula or the "evil twin" theme first explored in *Dr. Jekyll and Mr. Hyde* and likewise used to excess by those unimaginative soap opera writers. Bram Stoker and Robert Louis Stevenson can lay claim to popularizing, if not originating, those motifs. No, we're talking about the character not having died at all. Two of the greatest examples from literature have to be Tom Sawyer (who attended his own funeral) and Sherlock Holmes, who globe-trotted for three years before condescending to let his grief-stricken best friend know anything about it. Tom, a child after all, just lost track of time while playing pirates with Huck Finn. Holmes' approach seems harder to explain. Neither had amnesia.

At any rate, the reappearance of Sherlock Holmes was dramatic and exciting and truly spectacular. And if it worked for Holmes, there is no reason it could not work for others as well. Casting about the canon, more examples of reportedly dead men being alive after all easily can be found.

By far, the most colorful of these is Francis Hay (Frank) Moulton—documented to have been killed in New Mexico when "a miner's camp had been attacked by Apache Indians." Hattie Doran "never doubted that Frank was really dead," but her account of his reappearance in THE NOBLE BACHELOR rivals and even excels that of Sherlock Holmes, at least for timeliness and effect. Explains Hattie: "Frank had been a prisoner among the Apaches, had escaped, came to 'Frisco, found that I had given him up for dead and had gone to England, followed me there, and had come upon me at last on the very morning of my second wedding." Any modern soap opera writer would steal that scene in a minute! One of them probably has.

There are others. Henry (Harry) Wood, long presumed to be dead by the man who had betrayed him at the time of the Indian Mutiny, so shocked James Barclay that he fell over dead—"The bare sight of me was like a bullet through his guilty heart," said Wood in THE CROOKED MAN. The flint-hearted Jonas Oldacre of THE NORWOOD BUILDER hid in a secret room, trying to frame "the unhappy John Hector McFarlane." And Neville St. Clair was found in disguise, sitting in prison and accused of his own murder in THE MAN WITH THE TWISTED LIP.

All of these returned to the living in the very pages of the canon. But could there be others? Holmes' adventures chronicle a number of "deaths" which were never really confirmed, leaving a crack in the door for a return. Here, then, is a top ten list of "not hardly dead" characters, in ascending order of their likelihood to have really been alive after all:

#10—John Openshaw of THE FIVE ORANGE PIPS

Sherlock Holmes has been harshly criticized for sending the hapless John Openshaw out of his Baker Street rooms and into the waiting arms of the Ku Klux Klan. But what evidence is there, really, that the young man was killed? All the constable on duty heard was "a cry for help and a splash in the water." There was no account of anyone actually identifying the body. An assumption was made based only upon "an envelope which was found in his pocket." Openshaw told Holmes he was "armed," but there was no report of a weapon being on the body, nor did he have a struggle with his attackers. He had two warnings from Holmes fresh on his mind and ample reason to be on his guard anyway. Openshaw's death was more likely to have been an elaborate hoax, a staged death to divert his adversaries. And perhaps Sherlock Holmes was "in on it" all long.

#9—Harold Latimer and Wilson Kemp of T***he*** G***reek*** I***nterpreter***

The whole tale involving Paul and Sophy Kratides, Mr. Melas, Mycroft Holmes and the two villains Latimer and Kemp is so full of improbabilities and unexplained loose ends that Watson's supposition about the demise of the two kidnappers/murderers easily can be taken with a grain of salt. There can be little doubt that the entire episode was in reality a skirmish in The Great Game (as Kipling described it) of international espionage and power-politics intrigue that Mycroft Holmes was so deeply involved in conducting. The "curious newspaper clipping" suggesting that Sophy "came to be avenged" by stabbing the two men to death would be child's play for the Secret Service—British or otherwise—to manufacture. Nothing in this story can be taken at face value; and Sophy, Latimer and Kemp may well have played The Great Game for many years to come.

#8—Hudson and Beddoes of T***he*** G***loria*** S***cott***

Sherlock Holmes suspected that Hudson, the blackmailing sailor-turned-butler, was murdered by one of his targets, Beddoes (formerly Evans). The police believed just the opposite—that Beddoes killed Hudson and ran off with whatever money he could scrape together. The fact is, there is not one shred of evidence that either of them was murdered at all. Both simply disappeared without a trace, and "neither of them was ever heard of again." Once the elder Trevor was dead and the secret of the *Gloria Scott* was revealed, Hudson's hold on Beddoes was gone. If no murder occurred, these two either went their own ways or perhaps—being practical opportunists—even came to terms and began a new life of criminal conspiracy together.

#7—Leonardo the Strong Man of T***he*** V***eiled*** L***odger***

The strong man of the Ronder circus would have been a woman's fantasy under any circumstances, considering his "magnificent physique" and "splendid body;" but Eugenia Ronder was particularly susceptible to his charms because of her husband's cruelty. They conspired to murder Ronder and framed the circus lion for the crime, but not before Eugenia was maimed for life. She kept their secret until she read in some unidentified newspaper that "he was drowned last month when bathing near Margate." But how seriously can this report be taken? After all, Leonardo had "a clever scheming brain," and the likelihood of someone so physically fit drowning at a seaside resort would appear to be as slim as it would be ironic. No, Leonardo would be more likely to end seven years of looking over his shoulder by faking his own death.

#6—Captain James Calhoun of THE FIVE ORANGE PIPS

Captain Calhoun and his two accomplices supposedly met their just desserts when the sailing ship *Lone Star* of Savannah went down in "the equinoctial gales" of the Atlantic Ocean. Now, the Ku Klux Klan of the 1880s—of which Calhoun and his minions were members—was not the beer-guzzling, pot-bellied, knuckle-dragging, semi-literate trailer trash of today. These were fairly sophisticated conspirators who had journeyed overseas to commit two, and perhaps three, murders undetected until they already had departed for America. Even if the ship really sank—and the only evidence for that is a rumor about a piece of wood with "L.S." carved on it—there is no absolute assurance that Calhoun was on board. For all we know, he made it back to Florida and lived out his life as just another bitter ex-Confederate, shaking his fist at history.

#5—The Worthington Bank Gang of THE RESIDENT PATIENT

The members of the Worthington Bank Gang—Biddle, Hayward and Moffat—stalked and finally killed their former partner in crime Sutton (a.k.a. Blessington) to exact their revenge because he had turned evidence against them. "From that night, nothing has been seen of the three murderers by the police, and it is surmised by Scotland Yard that they were among the passengers of the ill-fated steamer *Norah Creina,* which was lost some years ago with all hands upon the Portugese coast, some leagues to the north of Oporto." Of all the vague and weak cases for justice-served-by-fate-at-sea (a recurring theme in this list and throughout the canon), this takes the cake. This trio had no past history of foreign travel, and there is no real evidence presented to justify the assumption that they were on board this vessel. Scotland Yard, perhaps embarrassed by its failure to close the case, may have seized on an otherwise unremarkable loss of a rickety old steamer to get the case off the shelf.

#4—Don Murillo of WISTERIA LODGE

Six months after escaping England, Don Murillo, "once called the Tiger of San Pedro," and his secretary Lopez "were both murdered in their rooms at the Hotel Escurial at Madrid," where they supposedly were registered under false names. But all that Inspector Baynes, Holmes and

Watson had on hand to convince them that "justice, if belated, had come at last" was "a printed description of the dark face of the secretary, and of the masterful features, the magnetic black eyes, and the tufted brows of his master." However, Murillo was, after all, "as cunning as he was cruel," and he had managed to elude the howling mobs of a general uprising in the country he had ruled for more than a decade. Despite being hunted, Murillo always "took every precaution," and he and Lopez managed to escape England altogether. Surely, such a Machiavellian figure easily could arrange a pair of murders in Madrid, cross a few palms among the local police and the press, and see to it that the "printed description"—along with the false conclusion it was intended to produce—found its way to Baynes.

#3—Jack Stapleton of THE HOUND OF THE BASKERVILLES

Watson, himself, admitted that there was "no slightest sign" of Stapleton as they searched for him in "the heart of the great Grimpen Mire." When Sir Henry Baskerville's missing boot was discovered along the treacherous path, Holmes assumed that Stapleton had it with him on the night of the final attempt on Sir Henry's life. Yet, the time of the boot's usefulness was long past—there were many opportunities for Stapleton to get better, and fresher, objects bearing Sir Henry's scent after he became a regular visitor to Merripit House. And why would he carry it around once he had loosed the hound? "There was much we might surmise" about the fate of "this cold and cruel-hearted man," said Watson. However, the assumption that he was "forever buried" in "the foul slime of the huge morass" has very little in the way of facts to support it. Rodger Baskerville, who had at least twice taken on false identities (as Vandeleur and Stapleton), may have found a new identity and a new criminal career far away from the gloom of Dartmoor.

#2—Tonga of THE SIGN OF FOUR

No more thrilling chase scene can be found in literature than that on the Thames when Holmes and Watson pursued Jonathan Small and Tonga, a fierce Andaman Islander, who were aboard the *Aurora*. As Tonga prepared a deadly poison dart for his blow-gun, Holmes and Watson fired their pistols. Tonga "whirled round, threw up his arms, and, with a kind of choking cough, fell sideways into the stream." As they "shot past," still in pursuit, Watson records that he "caught one glimpse of his venomous, menacing eyes amid the white swirl of the waters." The body was never found, and Watson assumed that it lay "somewhere in the dark ooze at the bottom of the Thames." Yet, the last time anyone actually saw Tonga, he was very much alive—dead or even dying people in the water don't have "venomous, menacing eyes." The "choking cough" could have been no more than an exclamation of anger or fear prior to a dive into the water. Tonga was being shot at, after all. And don't forget, he came from a strong water-oriented island culture. A dip in the Thames likely would have been child's play for him. With a primitive instinct for survival, in a bustling city like London with so many places to hide, and with a large number of ships available for stow-away, Tonga was an odds-on favorite not only to survive, but also to escape England altogether.

#1—Birdy Edwards of THE VALLEY OF FEAR

Of all the supposed deaths in the canon, that of Birdy Edwards is the most difficult to believe. This was a hardened, experienced and very professional detective, a master of survival. This was a man who infiltrated the infamous Scowrers of Vermissa Valley, dodged several attempts on his life, and braved the violence of the California gold fields. He twice lived under false identities—as Jack McMurdo and Jack Douglas—and engineered a magnificent deception, the apparent deaths of the entire Wilcox family. If not for Sherlock Holmes, he would have staged his own death at Birlstone House. Yet, we are asked to believe that he was "lost overboard in a gale off St. Helena," an almost passive victim of the agents of Moriarty.

Some have speculated that Holmes' near-obsession with the evil professor caused him to leap to a paranoid extreme in linking Moriarty to *The Valley of Fear* case at all. In fact, there is no real evidence of a connection outside of Holmes' own assertions along with both a "cipher" and a letter from the mysterious Fred Porlock—neither of which mentioned Moriarty by name. But why, indeed, would Moriarty agree to help a bunch of coarse ex-convicts from America, no longer wielding any criminal power or organization and out of money (which had been "spent like water" trying to save Boss McGinty and his stooges), in what, to him, was a simple case of revenge? Why would Moriarty's reputation need such a boost? Even Holmes had to acknowledge that Moriarty's involvement was "an absolute extravagance of energy."

It seems much more likely that Birdy Edwards, with the help of his wife Ivy, once again engineered a death—this time his own. Holmes spoke truly when he speculated that "it was well stage-managed." And if Holmes was a party to Edwards' plan, knowing in advance that he intended to put his pursuers off his track once and for all by staging this "accident" (as the cable-gram called it), then blaming Holmes' nemesis Moriarty was a perfect diversion.

Holmes was looking "far into the future." He knew a showdown with Moriarty was coming. In the meantime, if he managed to boost the professor's reputation as "the greatest schemer of all time" while helping a friend and ally in the fight against crime, then all the better. Surely, Edwards, like Holmes, lived to work for justice long after Moriarty supposedly ended his life.

Notes

Young Adventures and Old Cases

Summary

	Suitors & Husbands	Family Relations	Specialists
The Adventures of Sherlock Holmes	*Godfrey Norton* A SCANDAL IN BOHEMIA	*James Windibank* A CASE OF IDENTITY	*John Clay* THE RED-HEADED LEAGUE
	Percy Armitage THE SPECKLED BAND	*James McCarthy* THE BOSCOMBE VALLEY MYSTERY	*Neville St. Clair* THE MAN WITH THE TWISTED LIP
	Frank Moulton THE NOBLE BACHELOR	*John Openshaw* THE FIVE ORANGE PIPS	*John Horner* THE BLUE CARBUNCLE
	Mr. Fowler THE COPPER BEECHES	*Arthur Holder* THE BERYL CORONET	*Victor Hatherley* THE ENGINEER'S THUMB
The Case-Book of Sherlock Holmes	*J. Neil Gibson* THE PROBLEM OF THOR BRIDGE	*Gen. De Merville* THE ILLUSTRIOUS CLIENT	*Lord Cantlemere* THE MAZARIN STONE
	Prof. Presbury THE CREEPING MAN	*Col. Emsworth* THE BLANCHED SOLDIER	*Mr. Sutro* THE THREE GABLES
	Ronder THE VEILED LODGER	*Tom Bellamy* THE LION'S MANE	*Robert Ferguson* THE SUSSEX VAMPIRE
	Josiah Amberley THE RETIRED COLOURMAN	*Sir Robert Norberton* SHOSCOMBE OLD PLACE	*Nathan Garrideb* THE THREE GARRIDEBS

But is not all life pathetic and futile? This quotation is from the beginning lines of THE RETIRED COLOURMAN. Watson tells us: "Sherlock Holmes was in a melancholy and philosophic mood that morning. His alert practical nature was subject to such reactions."

("Young Adventures and Old Cases" was presented at *A Gathering of Southern Sherlockians* conference in Chattanooga, Tennessee, in April 2005.)

Trailblazers in the World of Ideas

Watson's fundamental misunderstanding of Sherlock Holmes. Morris Rosenblum touched on this issue as it relates to the misuse of the Horace quotation in his humorous article, HAFIZ AND HORACE, HUXTABLE AND HOLMES in *The Baker Street Journal* (Old Series), Vol. 1, No. 3 (July 1946), pp. 261-269. Rosenblum tried to make a direct connection among all three of the canonical references to Horace.

William S. Anderson. This quotation is from HORACE in *Academic American Encyclopedia* (Danbury, CT: Grolier, 1993), pp. 233-234.

L.P. Wilkinson. This quotation is from HORACE in *Collier's Encyclopedia, Vol. 12* (New York: Macmillan, 1989), pp. 242-244.

Roman lyric poetry that could stand beside the Greek. David West, Emeritus Professor of Latin in the University of Newcastle upon Tyne, expands on this idea among many others concerning Horace's life and work in his detailed introduction to *Horace: The Complete Odes and Epodes* (Oxford: Oxford University Press, 1997). West prepared the introduction and notes to his own well-crafted translation.

Horace was "short and fat." Seutonius wrote a brief "Life" of Horace. Physical descriptions of the poet come from that source, from Horace's own poetry, and from letters written by Augustus himself.

a marked Horatian influence. Another quotation from L.P. Wilkinson in *Collier's Encyclopedia.*

My Arrangement with Mr. Holmes

After all, he earned his fee. The story of Holmes' discovery of Neville St. Clair's secret identity is recounted in THE MAN WITH THE TWISTED LIP.

Persian slipper. "But with me there is a limit, and when I find a man who keeps his cigars in the coal-scuttle, his tobacco in the toe end of a Persian slipper, and his unanswered correspondence transfixed by a jack-knife into the very centre of his wooden mantelpiece, then I begin to give myself virtuous airs" (THE MUSGRAVE RITUAL).

You had no qualms about telling me you thought Neville was dead. The exact pertinent dialogue from THE MAN WITH THE TWISTED LIP is as follows:

> "Now, Mr. Sherlock Holmes . . . I should very much like to ask you one or two plain questions, to which I beg that you will give a plain answer."
> "Certainly, madam."
> "Do not trouble about my feelings. I am not hysterical, nor given to fainting. I simply wish to hear your real, real opinion."
> "Upon what point?"
> "In your heart of hearts, do you think that Neville is alive?"
> Sherlock Holmes seemed to be embarrassed by the question.
> "Frankly, now!" she repeated, standing upon the rug and looking keenly down at him as he leaned back in a basket-chair.
> "Frankly, then, madam, I do not."
> "You think that he is dead?"
> "I do."
> "Murdered?"
> "I don't say that. Perhaps."

letters transfixed to the wall with a knife. See the above note on the Persian slipper for the relevant quotation from THE MUSGRAVE RITUAL.

perhaps you have a low opinion of my sex. This was a perceptive observation from Mrs. St. Clair. Holmes did, indeed, have a fairly low opinion of women. "Women are never to be entirely trusted, not the best of them," said Holmes in *The Sign of Four.* Then there is this observation from him:

"The motives of women are so inscrutable. You remember the woman at Margate whom I suspected for the same reason. No powder on her nose—that proved to be the correct solution. How can you build on such a quicksand? Their most trivial action may mean volumes, or their most extraordinary conduct may depend upon a hairpin or a curling tongs" (THE SECOND STAIN).

("My Arrangement with Sherlock Holmes, by Mrs. Neville St. Clair" first appeared in *The Holmes & Watson Report,* September 2003).

Sightings at Twilight

That guy? Almost everything we know of Professor Moriarty, and the basis for virtually every descriptive reference in this piece, comes from THE FINAL PROBLEM and THE EMPTY HOUSE—stories which detail the death and resurrection of Sherlock Holmes—and *The Valley of Fear*. The perspective here is that of a young man who is wholly the product of the entertainment age.

A Night at the Roxbury. A 1998 film starring two regulars from *Saturday Night Live*, Will Ferrell and Chris Kattan, and directed by John Fortenberry. The Butabi Brothers are mired in the disco age, and their violent synchronized head movements are a running gimmick.

Young Frankenstein. A hilarious 1974 comedy spoof of classic horror films, directed by Mel Brooks. Peter Boyle as the monster has an extremely prominent forehead. The story was reincarnated in the 21st Century as a Broadway musical.

Lurch . . . the Addams Family. *The Addams Family* was the ghoulish group which served as the subject of a Charles Addams' long-running cartoon in *The New Yorker* magazine and, more famously, in a macabre but campy television series which aired 1964-66. Lurch was the looming, morose, and cadaverous butler.

The "nutty professor". *The Nutty Professor* was a 1963 comedy film starring Jerry Lewis as a nerdy college professor who is transformed into a suave and appealing man-about-town. Lewis was also the director. Remade in an interesting way in 1996 with Eddie Murphy as the star, directed by Tom Shadyac.

mom sitting in a chair in the basement . . . Remind me to lock the door the next time I take a shower. The reference is the classic 1960 thriller *Psycho* directed by Alfred Hitchcock. Norman Bates (Anthony Perkins) slices up Janet Leigh in the shower in one of filmdom's most famous murder scenes while his mother's skeleton waits for him in the basement. A truly unfortunate remake, directed by Gus Van Sant, appeared in 1998.

("Sightings at Twilight" first appeared in *The Holmes & Watson Report*, November 2000.)

A Chill on the Moor

a tale of twisted sex. *In Bed with Sherlock Holmes: Sexual Elements in Arthur Conan Doyle's Stories of the Great Detective* by Christopher Redmond (Toronto: Simon & Pierre, 1984), p. 10.

Césare Lombroso (1835-1909), was born in Verona, Italy. In his earliest writings, especially, he generally regarded criminals as a human "sub-species" and looked upon women and Africans as inherently inferior. Despite the odious and discredited nature of these particular ideas, because of his fundamental concept that certain factors can predispose individuals toward crime and his emphasis on the scientific method, he is still regarded as the "father" of scientific criminology. His views moderated somewhat over time to acknowledge social as well and physically inherited factors in criminal behavior. His book, *The Man of Genius* (1889) argued that artistic genius is a form of inherited insanity—which certainly has implications for Holmes' comments about "art in the blood." And like Conan Doyle, he apparently was influenced to some degree by spiritualism at the very end of his life.

Natural Born Killers. A hard-to-define but clearly satiric 1994 film written by Quentin Tarantino and directed by Oliver Stone crossing film *noir* with black comedy with some pretty damning commentary on modern attitudes toward celebrity.

Lord of the Flies by William Golding (London: Faber & Faber, 1954), an allegorical classic about the dissolution of civilization among a group of boys who have crashed onto a deserted tropical island. The competition between civilization and savagery among the boys reflects the same duality in individuals, families and society. Largely responsible for Golding's Nobel Prize for Literature (1983), the story has been filmed twice: a British version directed by Peter Brook in 1963; and a disappointing American version directed by Harry Hook in 1990.

Sands of the Kalahari. Another stranded by a plane crash film, this one from 1965 and directed by Cy Endfield, where the group struggles for survival and comes to resemble a nearby band of baboons. Stuart Whitman in the title role serves as an inspiration for the only marginally less ruthless contestants on the television series *Survivor*.

the lord of the manor taking a peasant girl. The *jus primae noctis* was the belief in feudal times that the lord of the manor had the privilege of sharing the wedding bed with his peasants' brides. In reality, it was probably actually practiced only rarely, but the very acknowledgement of the "right" was a method of keeping the peasants demoralized, dependent and submissive.

The Collector by John Fowles (London: Jonathan Cape, 1963). The 1965 film version, directed by William Wyler and starring Terence Stamp and Samantha Eggar, is one of those rare instances of the film matching the quality of the book.

Fowles . . . introduction to ***The Hound.*** Fowles actually wrote both a forward and afterword for a 1974 version (London: John Murray and Jonathan Cape), part of a collected edition.

this attitude toward animals in children. ANIMAL ABUSE AND INTERPERSONAL VIOLENCE by Suzanne Conboy-Hill, as it appeared on the Companion Animal Behaviour Therapy Study Group Website, February 2001. Also, THE TANGLED WEB OF ANIMAL ABUSE: THE LINKS BETWEEN CRUELTY TO ANIMALS AND HUMAN VIOLENCE by Randall Lockwood and Guy R. Hodge (*Humane Society News*, 1986), pp. 1-4.

Boy George . . . David Bowie, two British singers who became symbols of androgyny. Boy George (George Alan O'Dowd), born 1961, was the flamboyant transvestite singer for the ethnically-diverse band Culture Club. David Bowie, born 1947, first came to the public eye in 1969 and is a more serious musician, actor, record producer and arranger. Twice married, Bowie confirmed his bisexuality in 1972, but has backed away from that description of himself.

The Merck Manual of Diagnosis and Therapy (Fifteenth Edition); Robert Berkow, editor-in-chief; and Andrew J. Fletcher, assistant editor (Rahway, NJ: Merck, Sharp & Dohme Research Laboratories, 1987), p. 1499.

going bad, for a woman in the Victorian era, pretty much meant one thing: prostitution. For an outstanding study of this subject, *Prostitution and Victorian Society: Women, Class and the State* by Judith R. Walkowitz (Cambridge University Press, 1980).

the reckless rock star Madonna (Madonna Louise Ciccone), born 1958, a singer noted for her provocative and sometimes shocking erotic imagery.

Bantam paperback edition. *The Hound of the Baskervilles* by Arthur Conan Doyle (New York: Bantam Books, March 1949). The cover illustration by Bill Shoyer shows Stapleton tying an alluring and buxom Beryl to the post with sheets; a blurb at the front of the book describes the scene. This was an edition clearly designed to appeal to the pulp mystery fiction popular at the time of publication.

("A Chill on the Moor: Sex and Sadism in the Baskerville Line" was presented at *A Gathering of Southern Sherlockians: The Year of the Hound* in Chattanooga, Tennessee, in April 2009.)

Horror of the Hound

Holmes receives a visitor. This novelty poem has two aims, to provide a faithful retelling in verse of the entire story of *The Hound of the Baskervilles* and to begin every line with a different word beginning with "H." Excepting the refrain, which is similar (but not necessarily identical) in each of the five stanzas, only two lines begin with the same "H" word. Appropriately enough, that word is "Holmes."

("Horror of the Hound" first appeared in *The Holmes & Watson Report*, January 1998.)

The Rule of Three

The Victorian Vogue. The information in this section attributed to Thomas and Jean Sebeok and alluding to Charles Sanders Peirce is derived from *The Sign of Three: Dupin, Holmes, Peirce*, Umberto Eco and Thomas A. Sebeok, eds. (Bloomington/Indianapolis: Indiana University Press, 1988.) More particularly, the ideas are contained in Chapter 2: You Know My Method: A Juxtaposition of Charles S. Peirce and Sherlock Holmes by Thomas A. Sebeok and Jean Umiker-Sebeok.

in the image of God. "So God created man in his own image, in the image of God he created him; male and female he created them" (Genesis 1:27). *Revised Standard Version*, © 1952.

Where was the detective story until Poe breathed the breath of life into it? Martin Booth discusses Conan Doyle's "great debt to Poe" repeatedly in *The Doctor and the Detective: A Biography of Sir Arthur Conan Doyle* (New York: Thomas Dunne Books, 1997), pp. 104-105 and elsewhere.

blind beetles. Succinctly cited by Thomas W. Ross in *Good Old Index: The Sherlock Holmes Handbook* (Columbia, SC: Camden House, 1997), p. 24.

Little pig, little pig, let me come in. This particular version of the quotation is found in THE STORY OF THE THREE LITTLE PIGS from *English Fairy Tales*, collected by Joseph Jacobs, and contained in the wonderful anthology: *The Illustrated Treasury of Children's Literature*, Margaret Martignoni, ed. (New York: Grosset & Dunlap, 1955), pp. 80-82.

The Three Musketeers. This abridged passage is from *The Three Musketeers* by Alexandre Dumas as translated and arranged by Philip Schuyler Allen (New York/Chicago/San Francisco: Rand McNally & Co., 1923), pp. 280-283.

Double, double, toil and trouble. From *Macbeth* (Act IV, Scene 1) by William Shakespeare.

The Rule of Three. A good, brief and fairly understandable summary can be found in the Sherlockian's best and most reliable reference guide, *The Encyclopaedia Sherlockiana: A Universal Dictionary of the State of Knowledge of Sherlock Holmes and His Biographer John H. Watson, M.D.* by Jack Tracy (Garden City, NY: Doubleday & Co., 1977), pp. 310-311.

("The Rule of Three: The Significance of Sherlockian Trios" was delivered at *The 21st Annual Dayton Sherlock Holmes/Arthur Conan Doyle Symposium* in Dayton, Ohio, in March 2002.)

Deeper Shades

silk or brocade dressing or morning gowns were worn . . . with a tassel ended cord. From *History of Men's Costume* by Marion Sichel (New York: Chelsea House Publishers, 1984), p. 50.

A dressing-gown is actually defined. This definition comes from *Webster's New World Dictionary of American English: Third College Edition*, Victoria Neufeldt, ed. (New York: Webster's New World, 1988), p. 415.

Holmes had at least three dressing-gowns. So says Jack Tracy in *The Encyclopaedia Sherlockiana*, p.109.

S.F. Blake. Mr. Blake's ideas, one of the few articles dealing exclusively with this subject, are advanced in SHERLOCK HOLMES' DRESSING GOWN(S) in *The Baker Street Journal*, Vol. 10, No. 2 (April 1960), pp. 86-89.

Father Ronald A. Knox . . . actual inconsistencies. From STUDIES IN THE LITERATURE OF SHERLOCK HOLMES, which can be found in his book *Essays in Satire* (London: Sheed and Ward, 1928), pp.152-153.

convoluted assessment . . . by Christopher Morley. From WAS SHERLOCK HOLMES AN AMERICAN?, which can be found in *The Standard Doyle Company: Christopher Morley on Sherlock Holmes*, Steven Rothman, ed. (New York: Fordham University Press, 1990), p. 40 note.

Judge S. Tupper Bigelow. From THE BLUE ENIGMA, in *The Baker Street Briefs* (Toronto: Metropolitan Toronto Reference Library, 1994), p. 34.

More than anything, color has the ability to reveal a tremendous amount. This quotation is from YOUR TRUE COLORS ARE SHOWING by Rita Demontis (*Toronto Sun*, May 23, 1996), p. 69.

Martin Dakin considered the evidence. *A Sherlock Holmes Commentary* by Martin Dakin (Newton Abbott, Devon, UK: David & Charles, 1974), p. 69.

the blue dressing-gown belonged to Neville St. Clair. One of those who concurs with this view is Richard Lancelyn Green in EXPLANATORY NOTES for *The Oxford Sherlock Holmes: The Adventures of Sherlock Holmes* (Oxford, UK: Oxford University Press, 1993), p. 351.

people often match colors to their moods. From ON THE HOUSE by Susan Martin (*The Buffalo News*, Dec. 25, 1994), p. 3 of Lifestyles Section.

promote relaxation. From THE BLUING OF AMERICA: COLOR PSYCHOLOGY IS USED ROUTINELY TO MANIPULATE TASTES by Anastasia Toufexis (*Time*, July 18, 1983), p. 62.

blue can sedate the nerves . . . quieting color . . . calming effect . . . tranquilizing. One of the foremost modern authorities on color psychology is Dr. Morton Walker, an award-winning medical journalist and a prolific author. These citations are from his authoritative book, *The Power of Color* (Garden City, NY: Avery Publishing Group, 1991), pp. 17 and 52.

we are conditioned to seeing distances through a bluish haze. From WHEN COLOR PHOTOGRAPHS MAKE YOU SEE RED by David Brauner (*The Jerusalem Post*, Jan. 22, 1995), p. 7.

his second reference. That is, the second *published* reference. Although the blue and purple gowns were mentioned in published cases prior to any other reference to Holmes in a dressing-gown, several other mentions may have occurred earlier in a chronological sense.

a special Christmas present, say from Mrs. Hudson. Dakin, *A Sherlock Holmes Commentary*, p. 74.

brother Mycroft. These descriptions of Mycroft Holmes' physical and personal characteristics come from THE BRUCE-PARTINGTON PLANS and THE GREEK INTERPRETER.

a symbol of royalty and spiritual authority . . . costly to produce . . . the symbol of royalty. Walker, *The Power of Color*, pp. 17 and 25.

Judges 8:26 . . . Mark 15:16-20. *Revised Standard Version*, © 1952.

associated with the Roman monarchy . . . a synonym for the throne . . . worn on days of intercession . . . concerned with the Passion. From *Symbols, Signs and Their Meaning* by Arnold Whittick (London: Leonard Hill Books, 1960), p. 242.

official liturgical color for the season of Advent. From *Our Sunday Visitor's 1997 Catholic Almanac*, Felician A. Foy and Rose M. Avato, eds. (Huntington, IN: Our Sunday Visitor, 1997), p. 215.

violet can overwhelm a person. Walker, *The Power of Color*, p. 17.

E.J.C. This quotation is from COMMUTING A FELONY: AN OPINION FROM BRITISH COUNSEL by E.J.C. in *The Baker Street Journal*, Vol. 3, No. 3 (Old Series), 1948, p. 312.

a good practical knowledge of British law. As noted in Watson's catalogue of "Sherlock Holmes—his limits" in *A Study in Scarlet* (Chapter 2).

William S. Baring-Gould. The speculation about "royal blood in his veins" is found Baring-Gould's *The Annotated Sherlock Holmes: Volume I.* (New

York: Clarkson N. Potter, 1977), p. 467 note. An earlier use of the idea by the same author is found in the NOTES section of *The Adventure of the Speckled Band and Other Stories* by Arthur Conan Doyle (New York: Signet Classics, 1965), p. 276.

high-profile contentions to the contrary. Americans, particularly, would love to claim Sherlock Holmes. The most illustrious of those hoping for such a connection was President Franklin D. Roosevelt, who made the case in SHERLOCK HOLMES WAS AN AMERICAN!, which can be found in *A Sherlock Holmes Compendium,* Peter Haining, ed. (Secaucus, NJ: Castle Books, 1980), pp. 101-102. Christopher Morley had similar thoughts in WAS SHERLOCK HOLMES AN AMERICAN?, previously cited.

recalls the absolution offered by a Roman Catholic priest after confession. As noted by Richard Lancelyn Green in EXPLANATORY NOTES for *The Oxford Sherlock Holmes: The Adventures of Sherlock Holmes.*

Catholic doctrine . . . salvation comes from God alone. From the authoritative statement of Roman Catholic belief, *Catechism of the Catholic Church* (New York: Image/Doubleday, 1995), p. 52.

Michael Harrison . . . the nature of the Holmes wardrobe . . . 4 dressing-gowns From one of Mr. Harrison's numerous learned treatises on Sherlock Holmes: *Immortal Sleuth: Sherlockian Musings and Memories* (Dubuque, IA: Gasogene Press, 1983), pp. 87 and 101.

The simplest color for the eye to process is gray. Walker, *The Power of Color,* p. 66.

the color preferred by people who are indecisive. From PAINT COMPANY CODES SEXINESS BY FAVORITE COLOR by Angela Mangiacasale (*The Ottawa Citizen,* Feb. 24, 1996), p. I-3.

the word "mouse". The definitions cited for "mouse," both as a color and as a verb, are from *The Compact Edition of the Oxford English Dictionary* (Oxford, UK: Oxford University Press, 1971), pp. 718-719. Sherlockian scholars have accepted this exact terminology for the color—"dark gray with a yellowish tinge"—in a number of subsequent commentaries, including NOTES by Felicia Gordon and Richard Adams in *His Last Bow: The Heritage of Literature Series* (London: Longman Group, 1980), p. 213; and EXPLANATORY NOTES by Owen Dudley Edwards in *The Oxford*

Sherlock Holmes: His Last Bow (Oxford, UK: Oxford University Press, 1993), p. 188.

(*Deeper Shades: The Dressing-Gowns of Sherlock Holmes and the Psychology of Color* was privately published by the author as a monograph in 1998.)

Leading with the Chin

The Three Little Pigs. A good source for this tale is cited above, in notes for THE RULE OF THREE, although there are many versions commonly available (in appropriately sanitized versions) in children's anthologies.

Let me have men about me that are fat! From *Julius Caesar* (Act I, Scene 2) by William Shakespeare.

fall over the footstool *a la* Dick Van Dyke. *The Dick Van Dyke Show* was a highly successful situation comedy which aired on CBS from 1961 to 1966 and has been broadcast regularly in reruns ever since. A running gag during the opening credits for most of the series' run featured Van Dyke—known for his physical comedy—falling over a footstool in his living room. It is an enduring image of the television age.

("Leading with the Chin: Careful Considerations Concerning Canonical Chins" first appeared in *The Holmes & Watson Report,* November 2001.)

Dr. Sterndale, the African Explorer

Poldhu Bay. This site, whose actual name is Poldhu Cove, is an inlet on the eastern side of Mount's Bay, at the extremity of Cornwall. To be exact, it is about four miles from Lizard Point, the southernmost point of Great Britain. In 1901, just four years after the events in THE DEVIL'S FOOT, Poldhu Cove was origination point for the first trans-Atlantic radio transmission. The recipient, in Newfoundland, was the great radio pioneer Marconi. The preparations for this vitally important experiment would not have escaped the notice of Mycroft Holmes and the British government.

But exactly what kind of a doctor was Sterndale? Sterndale was, I think, a medical doctor, who, like the notorious British poisoner Dr. William Palmer, used his knowledge and training for more lethal purposes. Citing Palmer, who was hanged in 1856, Holmes observed in THE SPECKLED

BAND: "When a doctor does go wrong he is the first of criminals. He has nerve and he has knowledge." A medical doctor would just as easily be "the first of foreign agents" for the same reasons.

he *is* the British government. This famous assertion is found in THE ADVENTURE OF THE BRUCE-PARTINGTON PLANS.

Col. Sebastian Moran, whose story is told in THE ADVENTURE OF THE EMPTY HOUSE.

("Dr. Sterndale, the African Explorer" was the first half of the presentation "Hooray for Dr. Sterndale, the African Explorer" first presented at the *Holmes Under the Arch II* conference in St. Louis, Missouri, in May 2005.)

A Tale from the Crypt

he rejects the whole idea as nothing but rubbish. Despite Arthur Conan Doyle's obsession with Spiritualism in his later years, Sherlock Holmes never grappled with the paranormal in any of the original stories. Any of his cases with a ghostly premise, perhaps most notably *The Hound of the Baskervilles* and THE SUSSEX VAMPIRE, have perfectly logical natural causes and solutions, despite what initially might have appeared to be supernatural origins. The same, unfortunately, cannot be said for the stories involving another of Conan Doyle's creations, Professor Challenger, the hero of *The Lost World* (1912). In *The Land of Mist* (1926), Challenger and his associates become believers in, and even proponents for, Spiritualism.

***The Omen* or *Children of the Damned* or *The Bad Seed*.** Three films featuring murderous children. In *The Omen* (1976), directed by Richard Donner, little Damien Thorne is literally the Antichrist. In *Village of the Damned* (1960), directed by Wolf Rilla, and the sequel *Children of the Damned* (1964), directed by Anton Leader, children of a mysterious paternity have dangerous and fatal powers. (A remake of *Village of the Damned*, directed by John Carpenter, appeared in 1995.) In *The Bad Seed* (1956), directed by Mervyn LeRoy, an otherwise normal little girl is a heartless killer. (An unnecessary and inferior television adaptation of *The Bad Seed* was made in 1985.)

a wonderful definition of a "psychic vampire." "Re: Vampires" by Barbara Roden. In: *The Journal of The Arthur Conan Doyle Society*, Vol. 4 (1993), p.105.

Wes Craven, born 1939, the writer for a number of gruesome, graphic and particularly bloody horror/thriller films, most famously *A Nightmare on Elm Street* (1984) and its many sequels.

knowledgeable and accomplished expert. In his INTRODUCTION to *Dracula* (New York: Bantam Books, 1981), George Stade makes some interesting comparisons between Van Helsing and other fictional and real-life figures of the period. Says Stade: "Like his contemporaries Sherlock Holmes and Sigmund Freud, [Van Helsing] can solve mysteries and banish horrors that elude everyone else because he knows about them firsthand, from within . . . Again like Holmes and Freud, Van Helsing suffers from melancholia, but he also suffers momentary breakdowns into hysteria and something like madness."

the major characters themselves provide mirror images. George Stade, previously cited, had his own set of parallels for the Van Helsing character: "Van Helsing is to Dracula as Victor Frankenstein is to his monster, as Holmes is to Moriarty, as Dr. Jekyll is to Mr. Hyde, as Freud's ego is to his id. But he is also related to his author, with whom he shares a first name."

("A Tale from the Crypt: Unearthing Dracula in THE ILLUSTRIOUS CLIENT" appeared in an abbreviated form in *The Holmes & Watson Report,* May 2003. A much expanded version, with handout, was used for presentation at *Autumn in Baker Street,* in Norwalk, Connecticut, in September 2007.)

A Musical Toast to Nathan Garrideb

G-A-doubleR-I-D-E-B spells Garrideb. The chorus of this toast is a take-off on the song H-A-R-R-I-G-A-N, written by George M. Cohan in 1907 for the Broadway musical, *Fifty Miles from Boston.* It was most famously performed by James Cagney and Joan Leslie in *Yankee Doodle Dandy* (1942), a biography of Cohan directed by Michael Curtiz.

DeWaal. Ronald Burt DeWaal, the bibliographer of all things Sherlockian and compiler of *The World Bibliography of Sherlock Holmes and Dr. Watson* (New York: Bramhall House, 1974), and its successors, *The International Sherlock Holmes* (Hamden, CT: Archon Books, 1980) and *The Universal Sherlock Holmes* in five volumes (Toronto: Metropolitan Toronto Reference Library, 1994).

1895 is gone. An allusion to the famous poem "221B" by Vincent Starrett, originally published in 1942 by Edwin B. Hill in a now-rare pamphlet titled *Two Sonnets* and often reprinted. The poem serves as something of a "creed" for Sherlockians. It closes by noting that Holmes and Watson "still live for all that love them well: in a romantic chamber of the heart: in a nostalgic country of the mind: where it is always 1895."

("A Musical Toast to Nathan Garrideb" was delivered at the annual banquet of The Nashville Scholars of the Three-Pipe Problem in January 2009.)

Between the Lines

a romance between the two. By far, the guiltiest party in this myth-making about Sherlock Holmes and Irene Adler was William S. Baring-Gould, the author of three books which have been very influential in the Sherlockian world: *Sherlock Holmes of Baker Street: A Life of the World's First Consulting Detective* (New York: Bramhall House, 1962), *The Annotated Sherlock Holmes* (New York: Clarkson N. Potter, 1977) and *Nero Wolfe of West Thirty-Fifth Street: The Life and Times of America's Largest Private Detective* (New York: Viking Press, 1969). His basic thesis is that Holmes and Irene connected during the Great Hiatus of 1891-93 and produced a child who grew up to be none other than Nero Wolfe, the greatest of all armchair detectives. Wolfe, of course, was the creation of American author Rex Stout. Like much, if not most, of Baring-Gould's "biographical detail," there is not a shred of canonical evidence for the theory. He simply created it out of whole cloth. Because of his well-deserved popularity, his ideas enjoy a much-less-than-deserved degree of credibility.

Irene Adler. Almost everything we know about Irene Adler is derived from the very first Holmes short story, A SCANDAL IN BOHEMIA, which was originally published in 1891 and appeared in book form as the first of *The Adventures of Sherlock Holmes*. This was a fortunate occurrence as it set a familiar tone for, and the high standards of, all the subsequent Holmes tales. Quotes about her here are attributable to that story.

Third, she was dead. A credible and very successful attempt to explain away this death has been devised by Carole Nelson Douglas, who has written a series of novels featuring Irene Adler and her husband Godfrey Norton, beginning with *Good Morning, Irene* (New York: Tor Books, 1990). To her credit, Ms. Douglas does not attempt to fabricate a romance between Holmes and Irene. Instead, she makes Irene Adler Norton an outstanding, if flamboyant, detective in her own right—and the competition with Holmes continues unabated.

Holmes' ruminations on Maud Bellamy. The chief proponent of the theory of a Homes-Bellamy romance is Brad Keefauver, publisher of *The Holmes & Watson Report*, who tried to institute a movement to "replace" Irene Adler with Maud Bellamy as *the* woman, but seemed to gain few converts to the idea. This article first appeared in slightly different form in the November 1997 edition of Brad's journal as a response to his theory (pp. 28-32). He deemed it "a nice stopping place for the controversy" at that time. Even so, he promised only a temporary pause, adding that "this matter is far from finished."

one of Poe's neurotic narrators. In this case, the quote comes from the short story BERENICE (1835), which was included in Edgar Allen Poe's collection, *Tales of the Grotesque and the Arabesque* (1840).

The Book of Life. An article written by Sherlock Holmes, but derided by Watson, in *A Study in Scarlet*, Chapter 2.

not a young man. THE LION'S MANE was Sherlock Holmes' penultimate case and occurred after his retirement to Sussex. He would have been approximately 53 years old at the time, easily old enough to be Maud Bellamy's father.

a gibe and a sneer. Once again, a quote from A SCANDAL IN BOHEMIA, and the basis of most subsequent theorizing about Holmes' attitudes toward women.

("Between the Lines: Thoughts on Sherlock Holmes and Two Remarkable Women" first appeared in *The Holmes & Watson Report*, November 1997.)

Dead? Not Hardly!

Big Jake. A 1971 western, directed by George Sherman, in which John Wayne is summoned by his ex-wife (Maureen O'Hara) to pursue and punish a gang of kidnappers, led by evil mastermind Richard Boone.

Escape from New York. A 1981 futuristic thriller, directed by John Carpenter, in which Kurt Russell is summoned to rescue the President of the United States, who is being held in Manhattan, now a maximum-security prison.

("Dead? Not Hardly!" first appeared in *The Holmes and Watson Report*, July 2001.)

Index

Abbey Grange, The 57, 59
Adair, Ronald 62
Addams Family, The 33, 130
Adler, Irene 10, 116-117, 118, 119, 141-142
Advent 73, 136
Adventures of Sherlock Holmes, The 9-17, 127, 135, 137, 141
Adventuress 10, 116
Aeneid, The 21
Africa 61, 63, 92-98, 131
Agar, Dr. Moore 95, 96
Agra 86
Alfred the Butler 57
Amberley, Josiah 11, 12, 127
Amnesia 120
Amsterdam 109
Anderson, William S. 20, 128
Apaches 10, 121
Armitage, Percy 10, 11, 127
Atavism 35-36, 37, 39, 46
Athens 21
Athos 55-56
Augustus (Octavian) 21, 128
Australia 58
Austria 102, 103
Autumn in Baker Street 140
Axis Powers 61

Bad Seed, The 99, 139
Baker Street Irregulars 32
Baker Street Journal 73, 128, 135, 136

Ballarat 58
Bar of Gold 31
Bardle, Inspector 89
Baring-Gould, William S. 74, 136-137, 141
Barrymore 37
Baskerville, Rodger 37, 39, 40, 124
Baskerville, Charles 37, 39, 45, 48
Baskerville, Henry 37, 45, 49, 51, 52, 56, 124
Baskerville, Hugo 35, 37-38, 39, 40, 46, 48
Bates, Norman 130
Batman and Robin 57
Baynes, Inspector 123-124
Beddoes 122
Bellamy, Maud 13-14, 117-119, 142
Bellamy, Tom 13-14, 118, 127
Beauchamp Arriance 94
Berdella, Robert 41
Beryl Coronet, The 13, 14, 77, 127
Bible 37, 72
Biddle 58, 123
Big Jake 120, 142
Bigelow, S. Tupper 66, 135
Billy the Page 16
Birlstone 65, 125
Bisexuality 42-43, 47, 132
Bittern 40
Black Peter 19
Blake, S.F. 65, 76, 135
Blanched Soldier, The 14, 127

Blessington 58, 123
Blind Beetles 54-55, 134
Bloodline Theory 36-37, 46-47
Blow-Gun 124
Blue Carbuncle, The 15, 65, 66, 70, 72, 73, 85, 97, 127
Boccaccio, Giovanni 22
Bologna 22
Boone, Hugh 27, 30, 31, 90
Boone, Richard 142
Boscombe Valley Mystery, The 13, 21, 58, 60, 127
Boswell, James 22-23
Bow Street 26, 27, 29, 32
Bowie, David 42, 132
Boy George 42, 132
Boyle, Peter 130
Brackenstall, Sir Eustace 59
Bradstreet, Inspector 26, 30, 31
British Birds 63
Brooks, Mel 130
Browner, Jim 54
Bruce-Partington Plans, The 65, 67, 81, 82, 136, 139
Brunton, Richard 60
Brutus 21
Buddha 68
Buzzards 59, 60

Cain and Abel 37
Calhoun, Capt. James 58, 123
California 125
Camden House 63, 76, 78
Cantlemere, Lord 16, 127
Cardboard Box, The 54, 77, 100
Carruthers, Bob 58
Case of Identity, A 12, 19, 21, 127
Case-Book of Sherlock Holmes, The 9-17, 127
Catullus 63
Cedars, The 27, 29, 30, 32, 67, 81

Central America 59
Challenger, Professor 95, 139
Charles Augustus Milverton 86, 89, 103
Children of the Damned 99, 139
Christianity 22, 37, 54
Christmas 66, 70-71, 72, 73, 136
Christmas Carol, A 57
Clay, John 15, 127
Clegg, Frederick 41
Cocaine 57, 65
Cohan, George M. 140
Collector, The 41, 132
Copper Beeches, The 10, 41, 55, 87, 127
Coram, Anna 86
Craven, Wes 100, 140
Creeping Man, The 11
Croker, Captain 59
Crooked Man, The 121
Cushing, Sarah 100

D'Artagnan 55, 56
Dakin, Martin 68, 71, 135, 136
Damery, James 102, 105, 108, 111, 113
Dartmoor 50, 124
Dayton Symposium 134
De Merville, General 14, 108, 113, 127
De Merville, Violet 101, 102, 104-109, 112, 113
De Waal, Ronald B. 115, 140
Decameron, The 22
Devil's Foot, The 83, 92-98, 138
Dickens, Charles 57
Dictionary of the English Language, A 23
Diogenes Club 95, 96
Disappearance of Lady Frances Carfax, The 57, 80
DNA 35, 37
Dodd, James M. 14
Dogs 11, 82, 90
Doran, Hattie 121

Douglas, Carole Nelson 141-142
Douglas, Jack 61, 125
Dr. Jekyll and Mr. Hyde 37, 120, 140
Dracula 99-113, 120, 140
Dressing-Gowns 57, 64-84, 134-138
Dumas, Alexandre 55, 134
Dundee 58
Dupin, C. Auguste 54, 133
Dying Detective, The 55, 71, 87

Echo, The 18
Edwards, Birdy 61, 85, 86, 125-126
Empty House, The 36, 61, 65, 67, 76, 78, 79, 130, 139
Emsworth, Colonel 14, 127
Emsworth, Godfrey 14
Engineer's Thumb, The 15, 77, 127
Escape from New York 120, 143

Ferguson, Jacky 99
Ferguson, Robert 16-17, 127
Ferrell, Will 130
Ferrier, John 59, 60
Ferrier, Lucy 59, 60
Final Problem, The 61, 62, 65, 74, 77, 130
Five Orange Pips, The 13, 58, 121, 123, 127
Fleming, Ian 94
Florence 22
Fowler, Mr. 10, 11, 127
Fowles, John 41, 132
Foxhound 81, 82, 83
France 22
Fraser the Tutor 43
Freud, Sigmund 54, 100, 140

Gambling 12, 14
Ganges 86
Garcia, Aloysius 59
Garrideb, Nathan 16, 114-115, 127, 140-141

Gathering of Southern Sherlockians 128, 133
Genesis 54, 133
Gentry 10, 116
Germany 22, 116
Gibson, J. Neil 12, 127
Gloria Scott, The 70, 122
Gold 11, 31, 58, 93, 125
Golden Pince-Nez 86
Gonorrhea 23
Great Game 122
Great Hiatus 63, 66, 76, 77, 78, 80, 141
Greek Interpreter, The 36, 60, 122, 136
Gregson, Inspector 18
Grey, Miranda 41
Grimpen Mire 40, 41-42, 47, 52, 124
Gruner, Baron Adelbert 14, 91, 101-113

Hafiz 19, 23, 128
Harker, Jonathan 104, 113
Harker, Mina 101, 105-109, 113
Harrison, Michael 75, 137
Hatherley, Victor 15-16, 127
Hayes, Reuben 61
Hayward 58, 123
Heidegger 60-61
Hitchcock, Alfred 130
Holder, Arthur 12-13, 14, 127
Holdernesse, Duke of 60
Holmes & Watson Report, The 129, 130, 133, 138, 140, 142
Holmes, Mycroft 36, 70, 71, 72, 94, 95, 96, 122, 136, 138
Holmes Under the Arch 139
Holmwood, Arthur 109, 113
Holy War, The 63
Hope, Jefferson 18, 19
Hopkins, Stanley 57
Horace 18-21, 22, 23, 128
Horner, John 15, 127
Hotel Cosmopolitan 15

Hotel Escurial 123
Hound of the Baskervilles, The 35-47, 48-52, 56, 57, 77, 82, 85, 124, 132-133, 139
Howells, Rachel 60
Huckleberry Finn 101, 120
Hudson 122
Hudson, Mrs. 25, 26, 57, 64, 66, 71, 119, 136
Hunter, Violet 87
Huxtable, Thorneycroft 20, 21, 23, 55, 60, 87-88, 128

Illustrious Client, The 14, 57, 91, 101-113, 127, 140
In Bed with Sherlock Holmes 35, 131
Intermittent Heredity 35
Iran 61
Iraq 61
Italy 21, 22, 61, 131

Japan 61
Jesus Christ 62, 72, 73
John Barrington Cowles 100
Johnson, Samuel 22-23
Johnson, Shinwell 57, 109, 113
José the Man-Servant 59
Journal of the Arthur Conan Doyle Society 99, 139
Julius Caesar 21, 87, 138

Kattan, Chris 130
Kemp, Wilson 60, 122
King of Bohemia 86
Kingston 104
Kipling, Rudyard 122
Klein, Isadora 100
Knox, Ronald A. 66, 135
Kratides, Paul 60, 122
Kratides, Sophy 122
Ku Klux Klan 58, 121, 123

Lake, Leonard 41
Lancelyn Green, Richard 135, 137
Land of Mist, The 139
Lascar 30
Latimer, Harold 60, 122
Leigh, Janet 130
Leonardo, the Strong Man 12, 122-123
Leopold II of Belgium 94
Lestrade 18, 45, 46, 57, 63
Lewis, Jerry 130
Lewisham Burglars 59
Life of Samuel Johnson 23
Limits of Sherlock Holmes 18, 19, 136
Lion's Mane, The 13, 37, 89, 91, 117-119, 127, 142
Lombroso, Césare 36, 131
London 21, 27, 31, 53, 58, 61, 62, 67, 71, 92, 94, 96, 102, 103, 104, 110, 119, 125
Lone Star 58, 123
Lopez 59, 123-124
Lord of the Flies 36, 131
Lost World, The 95, 139
Lurch 130
Lyons, Laura 44-45

Maberley, Douglas 100
Maberley, Mary 16
Macbeth 57, 134
MacDonald, Inspector Alec 65, 89
Madonna 44, 132
Madrid 123, 124
Man with the Twisted Lip, The 15, 25-32, 65, 66, 67-69, 80, 90, 121, 127, 128-129
Margate 122, 129
Masochism 44-45, 47
Mathematics 33, 53, 59
Mazarin Stone, The 16, 79, 80, 127
McCarthy, Charles 60
McCarthy, James 13, 60, 127

McFarlane, John Hector 121
McGinty, Boss 125
McMurdo, Jack 125
McPherson, Fitzroy 89, 91
Melas, Mr. 60, 122
Mercer 57
Merck Manual of Diagnosis and Therapy 43, 132
Merrepit House 45
Michaelmas 38
Milady 56
Missing Three-Quarter, The 54
Moffat 58, 123
Money 10, 16, 19, 39, 67, 70, 96, 97, 122, 125
Montpellier 22
Moor, The 35, 38, 39-40, 41-42, 44, 47, 49, 50, 85, 95, 96, 131
Moran, Col. Sebastian 36, 63, 67, 76, 77-78, 79, 96-97, 139
Moriarty 33-34, 36-37, 61-63, 65, 77, 79, 103, 125-125, 130, 140
Morley, Christopher 66, 135, 137
Mormons 60
Morphy, Alice 11
Morris, Quincy P. 109, 113
Morstan, Mary 89
Mortimer, Dr. 36, 39, 44, 47
Mother Goose 54
Moulton, Frank 10, 11, 121, 127
Mouse-Colored 65, 66, 67, 75-83
Mouser 82-83
Murders in the Rue Morgue, The 54
Murdoch, Ian 37
Murillo, Don Juan 59, 123-124
Murphy, Eddie 130
Musgrave Ritual, The 60, 74, 129
Mystery of Marie Roget, The 54

Nashville Scholars of the Three-Pipe Problem 7, 141

Natural Born Killers 36, 131
Naval Treaty, The 77
New Mexico 121
Night at the Roxbury, A 33, 130
Noble Bachelor, The 10, 19, 121, 127
Norah Creina 58, 123
Norberton, Robert 14, 90, 127
North Korea 61
Northcott, Kate 100
Norton, Godfrey 10, 11, 117, 127, 141-142
Norwood Builder, The 121
Nutty Professor 33, 130

O'Hara, Maureen 142
Oldacre, Jonas 121
Omen, The 99, 139
Openshaw, John 13, 58, 121, 127
Openshaw, Joseph 58
Opium 15, 30, 90
Oxford English Dictionary 23, 82, 137
Oz 101

Parasite, The 101
Pedophilia 42-44, 47
Peirce, Charles Sanders 53, 133
Perkins, Anthony 130
Persian Slipper 26, 64, 129
Petrarch 21-22, 23
Philippi, Battle of 21
Pike, Langdale 57
Pipe 26, 28, 29, 31, 57, 64, 65, 68, 69, 70, 77, 90
Plissken, Snake 120
Poe, Edgar Allen 54, 118, 133, 142
Poison 97, 124, 138
Poldhu Bay 95, 138
Pondicherry 58
Porlock, Fred 125
Portugese Coast 58, 123
Presbury, Professor 11, 12, 127

Princeton 50
Priory School, The 20, 21, 55, 60-61, 87-88, 89
Problem of Thor Bridge, The 12, 127
Prostitution 23, 39, 44, 132
Prowling Gown 67, 79-81
Psychic Vampire 99-100, 139
Psycho 130
Purloined, Letter, The 54
Pycroft, Hall 55

Randalls 59
Rat Pack, The 21
Red-Headed League, The 15, 57- 127
Redmond, Christopher 35, 131
Reichenbach Falls 62, 63
Resident Patient, The 58, 77, 123
Retired Colourman, The 11, 127, 128
Reversion 35, 36
Roden, Barbara 99, 139
Roman Catholic Church 73, 74, 136, 137
Romania 102, 103
Rome 19, 21, 22
Ronder 11, 12, 86, 122, 127
Roosevelt, Franklin D. 137
Rosenblum, Morris 128
Ross, Herefordshire 21
Roundhay the Vicar 96, 97
Roylott, Grimesby 10, 11, 12, 37
Rucastle, Alice 10
Rucastle, Jephro 10, 11, 12, 41, 55, 87
Rule of Three, The 53, 59-62, 133-134, 138
Ryder, James 72, 73

Sadism 38, 39, 40-42, 44, 45-46, 103, 104, 106, 107
Saltire, Lord Arthur 60
Sands of the Kalahari 36, 131
Sawyer, Tom 101, 120

Scandal in Bohemia, A 10, 22, 86, 116, 127, 141, 142
Scotland Yard 27, 123
Scowrers 125
Scrooge 57, 115
Sebeok, Thomas & Jean 53, 133
Selden the Convict 37
Seutonius 128
Seward, Dr. John 105, 109, 110, 111, 113
Shakespeare, William 23, 57, 87, 134, 138
Shoscombe Old Place 14, 90-91, 127
Sign of Four, The 57, 58, 59, 65, 85, 89, 124-125, 129
Sikhs 58, 86
Silver Blaze 89, 90
Simpson, O.J. 22
Sloan, Hans 115
Small, Jonathan 58, 85, 86, 124
Smith, Culverton 55, 87
Smith, Violet 58
Solitary Cyclist, The 58
South Africa 61
Spain 22
Speckled Band, The 10, 37, 127, 137, 138-139
St. Clair, Mr. & Mrs. Neville 15, 25-32, 66-69, 75, 81, 90, 121, 127, 128, 129, 135
St. Helena 125
St. Oliver's School 42, 44
Stackhurst, Harold 118
Stamford 22
Stanley, Henry 94
Stapleton, Beryl 42, 44-46, 51, 52, 56, 133
Stapleton, Jack 35, 37, 40-47, 52, 56, 124, 133
Starrett, Vincent 141
Steiber, Peter 62

Sterndale, Leon 92-98, 138
Stevenson, Robert Louis 37, 120
Stockbroker's Clerk, The 55, 89
Stoker, Bram 101, 102, 103, 106, 113, 120
Stone, Oliver 131
Stoner, Helen 10
Study in Scarlet, A 18, 20, 21, 22, 23, 54, 59, 60, 75, 82, 85, 88, 104, 136, 142
Suicide 12
Superman 15, 101
Sussex 89, 99, 142
Sussex Vampire, The 16, 99, 100, 127, 139
Sutherland, Miss 12
Sutro, Mr. 16, 127
Sylvius, Count 79

Tarantino, Quentin 131
Tea 16, 26
Thames 124-125
Threadneedle Street 30
Three Blind Mice 54
Three Gables, The 16, 54, 57, 100, 127
Three Garridebs, The 16, 54, 114-115, 127
Three Little Pigs 55, 87, 134, 138
Three Months in the Jungle 63, 96
Three Musketeers 55-56, 134
Three Students, The 54
Three-Pipe Problem 57
Throwbacks 35-36, 37, 39, 40, 46
Tiger of San Pedro 59, 123
Tobacco 26, 68, 69, 80, 90, 92, 129
Tonga 124-125
Tracy, Jack 65, 134
Transylvania 102, 104
Tregennis, Brenda 93, 96, 97
Tregennis, Mortimer 97, 98
Trevor, Victor 70, 122
Turner, John 58

Uncle Jeremy's Household 100

Valley of Fear, The 61, 65, 77, 82, 85, 89, 125, 130
Van Dyke, Dick 90, 138
Van Helsing, Abraham 101, 103, 107-113, 140
Vandeleur 42, 43, 124
Veiled Lodger, The 11, 86, 122, 127
Vermissa Valley 125
Vernon Lodge 104
Vestigial Tail 35
Victorian Law 10, 73, 74, 93, 136
Virgil 21, 22
Vlad III Tepes 102-103

Walachia 102
Walker, Morton 69, 73, 78, 135, 136, 137
Wayne, John 120, 142
West, David 128
Westenra, Lucy 107-108, 113
Whole Art of Detection, The 84
Wilcox Family 125
Wilder, James 61
Wilkinson, L.P. 20, 128
Williamson 58
Windibank, James 12, 127
Winter, Kitty 106-107, 112, 113
Wisteria Lodge 59, 123-124
Wolfe, Nero 141
Wood, Harry 121
Woodley, Jack 58
Worthington Bank Gang 58, 123

Yellow Face, The 89
Yellow Fever 39
Yorkshire 43
Young Frankenstein 33, 130

Edwards Brothers,Inc!
Thorofare, NJ 08086
13 August, 2010
BA2010225